The

by

Jesse Berridge

This edition was published in 2015 by
Papermill Books of Essex, England
in association with
The Little Baddow History Centre
to mark the centenary of the arrival of Jesse Berridge
as Rector of Little Baddow.

The original edition was published by
Andrew Melrose Ltd in 1926
.

Jesse Berridge
1874 – 1965

Rector of Little Baddow
1915 – 1947

to
My Wife

Preface to the 1926 edition

That the following pages include incidents relating to abnormal experience is a fact that impels the writer to claim the indulgence usually accorded to imaginative fiction less than would have been the case, say, twenty years ago. The potentialities of the soul, the tenuity of the barrier set between average human experience and the realization of a state of existence under conditions loosely called 'psychical' or spiritual, the futility of setting limits or giving definition to 'personality' – these things, claiming ever a wider recognition, plead against the former relegation of all tales of mystery, or of tentative exploration into the unknown world, to the intellectual or fantastic lumber in literature, in which the semi-crazed, the hysterical, or the mere seeker of the thrill of the unusual, take a pleasure that is rightly suspect.

Apart from age or sex or temperament, the story of the soul of man would seem to imply a process of redemption – in its widest meaning – fulfilled through virtues, emotions, or actions, in accordance with the temporary and historical setting, and contributed to by the impelling power of the unconscious self that lies behind every human character.

The drama of events, however it may fill the stage with hero or villain, laughter or terror, is a matter secondary to the great process, the issue of which is 'yonder.' After all, it is no new doctrine, either to religion or philosophy or art, that we are 'strangers and pilgrims,' and that the clue to the mystery of being is that we have a destiny within the purpose of God.

This is a tale more than a philosophical novel; yet there is a type of mind that can hardly tell a tale without a sense of the mystical, and a type of reader to whom he appeals, as deep calls unto deep. It shall suffice to say that behind the present story has brooded the thought that what was of old a

Stronghold and a witness to divine things may become a peril to the seeker of the spiritual; that the venture of the soul, howsoever courageous, amid uncharted depths of spiritual experience, involves profound danger; and that there would seem to be no limit to the waywardness of religious enthusiasm.

For the rest, the tale has a seventeenth-century setting; for three hundred years ago the soul also had its potentialities and went a-seeking in matters political, psychological, and religious with opportunities afforded by the events of the time that had the additional force of novelty. The scene is laid in a remote part of Essex, in the parish of Little Baddow, and interest centres at either end of the high Ridge that runs between that village and Danbury.

One detail may be added as witnessing to the touching sense of compassion and understanding in the mind of Jordan Gyll: in the parish register, Marabella is recorded as owning the surname of Freeman.

J.B.

Little Baddow, June 1924

CONTENTS

BOOK THE FIRST: SEPULCHRE

BOOK THE SECOND: TRYST

BOOK THE THIRD: QUEST

BOOK OF THE FOURTH: THE ALTAR

BOOK THE FIRST: SEPULCHRE

Chapter I

THE CAMP

The great Ridge, more than a mile long, that lifts Essex's wastes like a bulwark to its lonely outlook over the distant blue hills and the waters and saltings of the Blackwater estuary, runs, with scarce perceptible depressions and risings, from Danbury in the south due north to Little Baddow. It bears, poised on the latter extremity, an ancient earthwork. The ground falls away, on all sides but one, from the circular wall, and from thence a great tract of country is visible. It is a lonely place, even now, though a farmhouse stands nearby. Bracken and ling, scrub oak, brier, twisted thorns, decayed willows, struggle in wild growth upon the uncultivated land, to die and rot and seek sepulchre beneath the fine gravel and silvery sand and loam whereof the undulating slopes and valleys are composed. Water stays suspended, in quiet little pools and marshy tracts, on the higher levels, or finds its way slowly amid the 'mares' tails' in the deep valleys, and the ground is perforated by numbers of rabbits.

'Warren' is the old name of the waste place. The woodpecker dips across it, the jays cry from the wood in the hollow land near by. The unresting wind beats upon it, and the sun rises upon it from over the hidden sea and lights it, swinging round to set above the town of Chelmsford, touching the winding river to silver and rose. The dark mists creep over Maldon and hang over it, suspended above the dripping tangle of verdure, or pass slowly above it in waves, driven by the slow wind or hurried by southerly gusts that liberate the rain that beats upon it and sets the brook, last remnant of an ancient glacier, murmuring.

The place is well-nigh changeless. A lord of the manor, in a time when they took thought for such things, planted firs and larches, enclosing them with an earthen wall, but even now their occurrence seems to be due to the operation of nature rather than to the purpose of man. Pathways form slowly, hither and thither, scored by the outcrop of the gravel, or marked by bright turf cropped by rabbits, winding among ling and bracken, but finally to end purposeless and deserted.

The circular earthwork has yielded to the generations and to the onslaught of the seasons with infinite slowness. The double wall tends to a certain roundness and smoothness, and to become at last identified with the ground out of which human hands originally reared it. The fierceness of the men that uplifted the Stronghold has been refrained by the inexorable purpose and patience of God. Of old it was the refuge of wild folk, with their crude weapons, their brown women and children, their cattle driven hither up the slope before the presence of strange raiders from the lower lands or from over seas.

And amidst the Camp they made a Sepulchre, a long barrow to house their dead. Athwart it they hailed their gods – the Sun, the Moon, the changeless constellations. A tryst in time of danger, a place of fellowship and mutual succour, a point nearest the open sky, an eyrie that brought great spaces and vistas into their eager consciousness; the place was a symbol in their wild lives, of religion, of communion, of security, of Death. From the shadows of the danger-haunted valleys, in times of need, they lifted up their eyes to the bare black rampart of the hilltop, from whence came their help.

Well-nigh three hundred years ago the double wall around the Camp was more defined than it is now, and the loneliness was greater. There was no farmstead near at hand, and the cottages that in later times crept up the hillside that runs in steep and stony declivity to the bridge over Chelmer, had not been built. Beyond the density of Scrub Wood to the north-east lay Tofts Manor, but the folk in it seldom came hither. Walls and ditch and barrow lay open to a quiet, almost windless night with the stars glimmering and wheeling in the sky, Orion and the Great Bear showing enormous. And amid the placidity there broke suddenly a new and sinister sound from the north-easterly quarter. It was late August in 1648.

The bent figure of a solitary man raised itself quietly from the longitudinal barrow in the centre of the earthwork. He appeared to be in the attitude of listening. Completely hidden in a long cloak that covered his head, allowing only a few straggling white locks of hair to escape from it, the man - in his obscurity - seemed part of the ground upon which he bowed. He put out his hands and felt with the hesitating gesture of one blind. He stood upright, listening, and yet not raising his useless eyes.

The sound of distant guns came to him; a stirring of the night, an unquiet murmur, pulsations indistinguishable as separate sounds, more defined shots, and a single and louder explosion. Birds began to be disturbed, and called, disquieted. Owls cried, and subdued rustlings and twitterings indicated restlessness.

Presently the far-off cannonading ceased, and utter quiet resumed. The man slowly bowed himself down again upon the barrow, and leaned himself upon a young oak that grew from it. He was meditating profoundly, there in the night, above the dead.

Chapter II

THE STRANGE WOMAN

At the southern end of the Ridge, just within the borders of Little Baddow parish, and on the western side of the slope that was clothed by the waste growths of Longwood, stood a small dwelling commanding a great view over the intervening low-lying land – toward Maldon on the east, and far beyond Chelmsford to the west, bounded by the Galleywood hills, yet more distantly on the extreme verge disclosing faintly a range, well-nigh twenty miles away, whereon was built the town of Burntwood.

The cottage stood solitary, a little way back from the track that crowned the Ridge, and its steep Essex roof and single twisted chimney could be discerned for miles. A small enclosure surrounded it, but the frequent passage of geese, seeking extended pasturage on the waste, rendered the barrier of little use beyond serving as a boundary-mark.

It contained but two rooms and an outhouse, and within the thatch birds and voles made innumerable nests. Primroses and violets brightened the sheltered corners of the enclosure in spring, and gillyflowers straggled under the wild apple and bullas trees that grew closely to the building, but the weeds and uncultivated growths invaded the place more and more boldly and with greater success, till it seemed that - at no distant time - there would be complete reversion to primeval waste, when the work of human hands would slowly fall and perish and become one with the decayed leaves and sandy loam.

Few folk went thither, though the cottage was inhabited. Such as passed along the Ridge mostly had unquiet thoughts as they looked at the house. The surmises and judgments of the countryside gave a sinister colour to the place and the woman who lived there; and the dwelling itself seemed to bear the stain their thoughts set upon it. Down in the village they knew her as Marabella, and such was her name; heathenish and outlandish amid so many taken from the Word of God – Priscillas and Faiths and Graces and Mercys. They knew her too as 'The Strange Woman,' a name that contained a shameful accusation. Such few as would speak with her, for the sake of bargaining for geese or goats, did so unobserved; and she herself took notice of none, wrapped in her own concerns.

She came out quietly under the darkening sky and, leaning against the door, looked at the slender red crescent of the moon impassively. Her slight figure and her movements indicated that she was quite young. Her black hair curled to her shoulders and shrouded her black brows. The dark eyes, red lips and clear brown skin suggested foreign or gipsy blood, and were unusual amid the descendants of the East Saxons. She was clothed in grey bays, such cloth as might be bought at Braintree or Colchester, and her neck was open. Her bare legs and feet, brown and weathered, showed that she was used to doing without either stockings or shoes. She stood there at the door of her cottages and gazed at the red moon, her face expressionless and beautiful.

A sound of shambling feet and heavy breathing came from the back of the hut, and an undersized, almost misshapen lad appeared. His limbs seemed almost out of control and he leaned upon a holly stick. His splayed feet were bare, as were his legs to the knees. He was clothed in rough breeches of fustian and a sort of surcoat - made simply like a tabard with a hole at the top through which his shaggy head was thrust. A thatch of straw-coloured hair shot forward over his face; his eyes were narrow and without lashes, and his mouth, with thick lips, hung open habitually. He flung down upon the ground a dead rabbit, whose neck he had just broken with his great hands, and looked up at his half-sister for approbation. She scarce noticed him, and he moved awkwardly about within, blowing the ashes of the peat and talking to himself.

13

"Be the geese safe fro' foxes, Abel?"

"Ay, Marabella, an' the wood split, an' the water gotten – I be weary." He sniffed and looked at her wistfully.

She surveyed him with calm domination. "Go then," she said tonelessly.

He turned with awkward alacrity and made for the outhouse. There were subdued sounds as of straw rustling and broken soliloquy – then quiet, followed by heavy snoring.

The evening darkened and the hills beyond the distant estuary merged into the dark sky. A few stars showed. Marabella raised her arms and pushed the close hair from her brows. She sat within the hut now, upon a low wooden stool, leaning her head against the oaken jamb of the door, her hands clasped in her lap. The world became somehow airless and portentous. She closed her eyes.

Suddenly she looked out into the shadows without stirring – a slight sound had detached itself from all else and was forcing itself, insistent, into her consciousness. It was the footstep of one that was passing along the Ridge. With great deliberation it approached, sometimes hesitatingly, sometimes accompanied by the sound of a scratching or of a stick thrust against stones and thorns. It was well-nigh opposite the cottage now, and the girl clutched her brown throat to prevent herself crying out. A thrill of fear passed over her body and set her skin tingling, while a sort of nausea followed a momentary arrest of her heart's beating.

"Billy Blind!" she whispered dreadfully to herself; "Billy Blind!"

She remained motionless, and the steps passed on northward, deliberate, hesitating, yet unstaying. Soon they were out of hearing.

Marabella closed the door and set a wooden bar across it; then with quiet, trembling hands, she hung a rush screen over the single small window. Then she crouched over the peat fire, though the place was sultry and oppressive, and stared at the red glow. Her thoughts went back, called to the past by the sound of the strange footsteps.

She saw herself as a child, unkempt, uncared for, staring at the fire even then, with her bare legs and toes thrust towards the warmth, crooning a meaningless song and patting the ashes into shapes. The smell of the wood came back to her and the odour of the foul pot, with the stew that steamed from it, hanging from the chimney.

The witless old woman she had been taught to call 'Grandam' sat all hunched up, ruminating with bright eyes that were like those of a reptile, restless, meaningless, beneath scant hair and a great cap that covered innumerable wrinkles and uncleanliness. The girl saw again the perpetually moving hands that travelled the length of the hem of a tattered apron, the finger and thumb of one hand following closely the finger and thumb of the other; then, the end being reached, the reverse journey being made to the other border, and so on, the process endlessly repeated - for hours, for days, for weeks....

She remembered the wattle-and-daub hut close by the river on the track that went to Hatfield over the ancient ford, the sound of the water, the floods that rose and came close, the murmur and roar of the mill, the humming of the wheel. She recalled the same sound those eleven years ago that sent cold terror through her now, and the dialogue, repeated Heaven knew how often, after the darkness had fallen. The old woman that had scarce moved for hours except for her awful repetition of the hands upon the apron's hem, would slowly put her head on one side, her seamed face with something like an expression on it. The deliberate, hesitating step accompanied by the thrusting stick would pass up the hill, the child's hands and feet would become motionless, and the grandam's head would turn slowly.

"What's yon, Marabella?"

"Billy Blind, Grandam." So the dialogue would go without variation, in the Essex sing-song intonation; the old woman querulous and grimacing, the child listless and mechanical.

"Where's 'a goin' then?"

"Warren, I do reckon."

"What for to do?"

"Doan' know." And then silence while the footsteps died away, the old head slowly went into its former position, the child's feet and hands played among the ashes again, and the withered fingers of the old woman followed one another up and down the apron hem.

How many times had that happened on quiet or wintry nights in the past, ere the girl's sole protector died, without telling her of the father or mother she had never known; the old grandam living without thought or anxiety upon the pity of neighbours and bounty of the parish vestry, with these two gaining what scraps they could – the girl with the black eyes, the dwarfish elf of a half-brother well-nigh naked and dirty. The days came back to her, spent in foraging for drift-wood from the river, moor-hens' eggs from the bank, blackberries or wild apples from the common – a strange meaningless succession of days and nights that succeeded one another, the old woman growing more and more witless and helpless, the boy more brutish, till she had beaten him. But those nights, and the steps without, passing up the hill. They came back with a sudden intensity of remembrance as she cowered there, her lips apart, her eyes wide. The oft-repeated dialogue moved monotonously in her mind. She heard again the quiet fingers moving, the old woman's head turning, her own self at pause by the ashes. The very tones of her grandam's voice seemed to live again in her mind – the sing-song Essex talk.

"What's yon, Marabella?"

"Billy Blind, Grandam."

"Where's 'a goin' then?"

"Warren, I do reckon."

"What for to do?"
"Doan' know."

Chapter III

FROM THE DEAD SEA

The girl broke from her reverie with a sudden effort. The past began to live with an uncanny intensity in her mind, evoked by the sound of the footsteps. The impressions and incidents reiterated themselves in her mind unbearably. She shuddered, threw sticks on the fire, crouched before it, her dark beauty in strong light and shadow, the leaping shadows running up the wall behind her and the irregular rafters above her. Her restlessness soon wore away and she fell into reverie once more; a softer look came over her face and her fingers twined themselves together nervously.

She saw herself now as a girl of seventeen, and the face and the voice of Jordan Gyll seemed to fill the darkness above her. He had loved well, there was no doubt of that; his honest and open adoration was clear to the village, most of all to the lad's mother, whose bitter hostility to the nameless girl had at last found its objective. She recalled her own tremors and instinctive coyness; her waywardness, her purposeful retreats as he advanced his love, her proud assertion that if she were not good enough for Dame Gyll she was not good enough for her son; the repeated assurance from Jordan that he would break with his mother, and they would seek together a new life as soon as the grandam was beyond her helping. Well, it had been sweet while it lasted. She had felt so much wiser than the lad, knew him, as she thought, through and through, and the possibility had been before her for a short while that there might be a realization of what he desired for them. Not the roseate heaven his passion pictured, but still heaven of a sort, compared with the bleak and dark poverty, the witless senility of the old woman, the scorn of neighbours who had names – decent names and families belonging to them, and not a single heathenish word, come none knew whence. The possibility had floated before her, a coloured bubble upon the air. She knew almost as she considered it, that it was too fragile and dreamlike for realisation – and it had burst. Her own hands had destroyed it.

The footsteps that had been the strange background to the sordidness and squalor of her early life, formed also the beginning of a chain of events that ended in disaster.

They had talked, the boy and the girl, by the rail of the old mill one evening, and the sound of the lonely pedestrian came to them, approaching from the Hatfield bank. The old man had passed, unnoticing and unnoticed, a vague shrouded figure with a staff, groping this way and that, and picking at familiar landmarks – grass, buttress, or ditch – with such accuracy that it seemed difficult to believe in the blindness that common report gave to him. They had held their breath as he neared them; and when close, he had paused for the fraction of a moment, as though aware of their presence – even now, looking back, she felt again the thrill of that instant – and then he had passed into the darkness.

"Why do they call 'un 'Billy Blind,' Jordan?" she had asked.

" 'Tis a sort of hobgoblin, parson do say. None know'th the real name of him; but that he cometh from Witham way and goeth to Warren Hill and back o'nights."

"I be feared o' he."

"Then I will kill 'un, for making thee feared, if thou wilt…. Leave talking of 'un…. Wilt kiss me wi' free will, or do I make thee?"

"Nay, loose me. Wilt never kiss thee more, unless thou find out about Billy Blind – what he doth o' Warren Hill."

'Little fool, what care I what a' doth? Crazed he is, sure, ask parson else."

"Thou know'st parson is no friend of mine. They presbyters do scowl at me, as though they hated me for being what God made me – 'Marabella, Marabella; bitter and beautiful art

thou!' said parson… and shook his long back sleeves at me…
See, I will kiss thee, if thou follow Billy Blind, and if not, then I
will hate thee for a coward."

"Nay, dear child, what folly is this?"

"Then go back to thy mother… She will kiss thee in the
stead of me, and miscall me, and let thee hold the flax and
work the distaff!"

She had thrust the lad away with sudden violence, and had
run up the road.

In a moment he had followed her, unable to endure the
thought of her displeasure.

"Nay, I will do it," he panted as he overtook her. She
stopped, irresolute, suddenly averse to the thing.

"Well, then, I will kiss thee, and thou need'st not go. Truth,
I am somewhat of a fool; and thou art brave." She put her
hands on his shoulders, and a sudden doggedness came over
him. In his turn he put her from him.

"Shall see if I be coward… I will not kiss thee now, but after
I have done what thou say'st, then will I," and he turned
resolutely up the track away from her, while she stood with her
vague misgivings.

And then it was as though a power external to herself –
resistless, ungovernable – possessed her. She longed for him,
body and soul. She was part of him and he of her. She cried
wildly.

He came back, caught and held by the new sound of her
voice. With darkly flushed face he clasped her there in the
scented night, and she hung upon him, yielding, terribly
desirable…

Marabella, recalling these things, covered her hot face and
moaned softly to herself. Long past weeping, her eyes shone
hard and bitter. She would madden herself, as she knew, were
she to dwell in thought upon that night.

He had gone from her at length, and she had crept back,
with a strange and terrifying sensation of newness in her being,

20

to find her old grandam heedless of the passing of the hours, seated there, with her fingers restlessly, ceaselessly, employed. The fire had sunk to ashes, and the dawn was not far off.

The day passed, and the following night, without sign of Jordan. And then came the mother, a figure of wild wrath and hot denunciation, with stinging words demanding her son.

"Thou black, gypsy light o' love, where's my lad, my Jordan?"

Marabella had gloomed and flamed back upon her, silent. The eyes of the elder woman pierced her, and seemed by feminine intuition to discover the answer to her searching look. The girl's eyes fell.

"Jordan," cried the mother. "Child of my body, come thou forth from the house of yon strange woman, whose feet take hold on hell!"

There was dead silence, and Dame Gyll flung her hands out. She became inarticulate from passion. Finally she went, cursing.

Marabella had returned to her grandam, who was utterly unaware of what had been happening. She covered the old woman mechanically with a cloak about her head and shoulders, and pondered. Jordan, then, had gone from home.

Her thought passed on from the stopping-place of dire realization of his departure, to a fragment of conversation overheard by her, as she lay hidden below the bridge on a day a week later, when she had walked in the water by the river brink. Hearing someone approach, she had hidden herself. Two men were speaking quietly. She soon recognised the voice of the parson, and the man answering him was apparently speaking with reluctance.

"None but I do know, parson. But A cudden' keep 'un to myself. He did come runnin' like the swine of Gadara down the slope to where I did tend thy yows by the mill-stream. Devil-possessed he were, if ever I did see any so. I called out, 'Jesu save 'ee, Jordan lad!' and 'a threw 'un's arms about, and cried, 'Never will He again, Dickon! I have seen hell open, and I am a lost soul!' Then 'a plunged, clothes and all, into the water, and A thought 'a was gone for good, but 'a swam like a water-rat, and gat him out all a-drippin' and staggerin' on the Hatfield side... Crazed for sure, and dead by now, should say. Thowt they might say I'd ha' killed he, so A said nought to any...." She had heard no more.

She remembered the slow horror that seized her there in the dark shadow of the bridge. What had happened to her lover? Was the gift of her love the poison that had destroyed him?

Then she had recalled his determination to follow the strange figure that passed by night. Had he fulfilled that wild purpose to which she had urged him? She had never been able to answer the question. Jordan Gyll had gone from her life. She had never seen him again....

So the scenes, deeply impressed on her girl's mind, repeated themselves after the passage of six years, awakened by the noise of passing footsteps. She listened now, but without the house the darkness held scarce a sound. Near by, a crackling and rustling of straw indicated that Abel was turning himself in the little outhouse. His breathing, slow and regular, followed upon the sound of his movements.

And then a perplexing dream that recurred more than once to Marabella, obtruded itself. She had a horrible conviction that somehow it corresponded to truth, however she told herself that it resulted from her fears.

She had thought in her dream that she stood observing Jordan's steady tracking of Billy Blind up the hill. She watched both with a curious detachment. The mysterious figure of the sightless man persistently moving up the rough path, his head bowed, the grey locks escaping from a hood, his staff in ceaseless motion; Jordan some distance behind, cautiously ascending in his tracks. The dream obscured them, and then lifted its curtain, as it were, upon another tableau. The scene was now the old camp. She could know, rather than see, the ramparts of builded earth circling the long barrow. She felt the great spaces, the wilderness of gorse and bracken and oak and brier that spread downwards in shadow.

Her attention was fixed upon the barrow, for there was a figure bowed before it, and it was illuminated by a pale lambent flame that spread above it like a luminous plane with living pulsing fires within it. The figure of Billy Blind raised itself, and now, almost for the first time, she saw his face. She knew somehow that those eyes could see. They were searching the pool of light. She tried to call out, but the paralysis of dream strangled her utterance. Jordan was watching the portent somewhere there; she knew it, and she agonized to warn him, but could not. She saw the old man turn slowly with a sort of triumph in his new-found power of sight and look at Jordan, who cried wildly and fled headlong into the night.

Thus the dream had come not once, nor twice, and she feared sleep now, unless she were wearied out, when exhaustion would induce a profound unconsciousness.

She rose from her memories and her dreams and looked out into the night. She would think no more of the past, a Dead Sea whence came such bitter fruit. Far away to the north-east a spark of light attracted her notice. She was puzzled at its position. It was apparently from the half-ruinous palace, some five miles away on the crown of Wickham Hill, the former seat of the Bishops of London; half-stone, half-brick, tree-encircled, gloomy, dominating; now with its glory passed and its lords suppressed. She shaded her eyes and strained her sight into the darkness. Suddenly the light went out.

There was a little cry from the room behind her, where she slept. She went softly across to her inner door, lighting a taper on the way. A little boy of about five was sitting up on a rough pallet. His hair, fine as spun gold, was tumbled, his face flushed with sleep, but his eyes were wide and alert. He held up a finger to her, as though to bid her be silent, and remained in an attitude of one listening intently.

Chapter IV

WICKHAM BISHOPS

Little remained in 1648 of the moated palace on the crown of the hill at Wickham. A wild ruin of masonry, over which the brier trailed and the ground elder spread, covered the site that had once been the scene of ecclesiastical grandeur. The Bishops had been suppressed, the Church of England serviced abolished, and Presbyterianism took hold upon Essex. The palace had been dismantled, and much of it had gone to furnish material for other buildings. Folk avoided it, and there were rumours that it was haunted. The fragment of one wing still stood, overlooking a great tract of country, and signs were not wanting that there were mysterious happenings which the village knew of, but of which they would say nothing.

Strangers had been seen in the village: a pedlar, selling nothing; an old woman with hands and feel large enough for a man; soldiers of non-descript uniform – but that was not unexpected, with the siege of Colchester drawing to a close now, twenty miles away.

Yet these comings and goings had their cause in a singular and clandestine meeting in a lower room of the palace wing that still stood. It was closely curtained, and contained a makeshift altar, set with a crucifix, white cloth, and two lighted candles; on the north side of it was seated a pale, bearded man, habited as a bishop in rochet and lawn, tippet and square cap. Before the altar knelt six other men, four of whom had full surplices and cassocks over their clothes, and two had none, but showed signs of hasty dispensing with disguises. They had come hither singly, and at different times, by night, for the purpose of being secretly ordained to the diaconate, or priesthood, of the Church of England.

A server entered quietly through a thick door that was guarded on its outer side by an armed man. The Prayer Book and several Bibles were set down; a cushion was placed on the altar and the Ordinal opened. The vessels for the Eucharist were placed in the midst and covered; and the sacred elements were put within reach. The Bishop rose from his chair and surveyed the group. Then he whispered a word to the server, who retired again through the door, and a pause ensued. The six men remained at prayer.

At length a shuffling sound proceeded from the door. The server entered once more, leading by the arm an old priest, vested. His face was like pallid wax with innumerable lines about the corners of the mouth and eyes. Long white locks fell about his neck to his shoulders. His eyebrows jutted, and his nose was fine and delicate. His lips were closely pressed and his whole expression was that of infinite patience. His eyes were of a beautiful blue, and they looked motionless straight in front of him. At the door, the server let go his arm for an instant. The old priest walked on and encountered a piece of furniture, which he overthrew. It was evident he was quite blind.

He was conducted to the altar, touching things vaguely as he went – a table, the head of one of the kneeling ordinands, the frontal of the altar. He made a reverence first to the altar, then to the Bishop, and then was led to a seat on the south side. With a gesture he began:

"Reverend Father in God, I present unto you these persons present to be admitted as deacons and priests."

The service went on quietly. It was a strange scene, but by no means uncommon. Secret ordinations went on, despite the oppressive enactments that forbade them. The sentry moved about in the next room, jingling and scraping. The Litany and the *Veni Creator* were said, and the Eucharist followed. The old priest came forward and laid his hands, together with those of the Bishop, upon the heads of the newly ordained priests. At the conclusion of the service he went to the Bishop, who put his hand round his neck affectionately.

"God bless thee, Walter. Take heed to thyself and to the doctrine."

The old priest paused in a moment's thought, bowed before the Bishop, and retired as quietly, led by the server. The party broke up and shared a meal in the adjoining room. Presently they dispersed at different times, having resumed their disguises. The old priest, whom the Bishop had called Walter, bade them farewell one after another, standing at the door of the dismantled room that gave on to a broken stone stairway, from the foot of which they mounted or went on foot down the hill towards Maldon or Witham.

The last to go was a young man who had been ordained priest. He was now habited as a pedlar, and was taking his way to Maldon on a secret matter, and thence to the great house of Skreens, where he was assured of a welcome and a measure of protection from Sir John Bramston. He had come through deep waters ere he had offered himself for training and ordination in the proscribed Church. But his heart was uplifted with some assured sense that his penitence was availing, and his gifts, such as they were, would be used by the Giver.

It was afternoon when he strode down the slope. At a point in the road he stopped. Along the horizon spread the Ridge, violet and rose-coloured. He took note of Danbury church, and slowly, against his will, his eye travelled along it till it rested upon the northerly extremity. For years he had not seen it, for he had arrived by night. A troubled look came over his face and perspiration stood on his forehead. He looked intently, trying to discern the outlines of the hill, but it was too far to see details. He sat down and groped for his New Testament, given him at his ordination. To his dismay he found he had not got it with him. He had left it behind at the old house. After a moment's irresolution he strode quietly up the hill again. He arrived at the palace and was passed in by the sentry with a curt nod. A few minutes' search put him in possession of his book and, having secured it, he made his way quickly down the slope once more. This time he did not stop to survey the Ridge, but hurried on. At the foot of the hill the distances were hidden by trees. Now he walked more freely, his pack swinging behind him.

Suddenly, moved by impulse, he turned to look his last at the ruinous palace where he had received his Orders. The sun was westering and a red light fell upon the stairway he had himself descended a while before. As he looked, a small bowed figure appeared at the doorway. The young man stared violently.

The figure was that of an old man covered with a hooded cloak, from which escaped white locks. A staff was in his hand, with which he thrust this way and that. He moved deliberately, hesitatingly, unrestingly.

"Mercy of God!" whispered the young man to himself, "Billy Blind!"

Chapter V

THE ABYSS

Marabella stayed, arrested by the child's gesture. For a while she heard nothing, and then she heard a slight shaking of the little leaded window. She listened more intently. Far away there rose, slowly, the deep, reverberating sound of guns. It seemed at times more like a motion of the disturbed air and a pulsation of the earth beneath them, but at times definite explosions of heavier ordnance detached themselves from the distant cannonade. She knew now it was not the sound of tempest, but the besiegers of Colchester opening fire on the helpless town.

She moved toward her child and soothed him, whispering words of comfort. Her hard, bright beauty took a haunted look as she sat beside the pallet and watched him close his eyes. The child's hand, flung out towards her, seemed to possess a piteous appeal. The tossed limbs seemed so small, so defenceless. The delicate curve of cheek and chin, the lashes that glinted, the tumbled fair hair, all made a picture that she wondered at and loved, till her emotion became a pain.

Soon the breathing became regular, and the mother passed quietly back to the flickering light of the larger room. An intolerable restlessness invaded her. The past had swept back upon her and challenged the hardness and bitterness that she had assumed as a defence. The unconscious loveliness and tender appeal of the child denounced her silently. She stood with clenched hands and surveyed the dark outline of the trees without. The distant rumbling continued at intervals.

Her nature became insurgent. Wrong had been done to her, that she knew, though she was unable to discriminate or apportion blame. Her thoughts became a maddening circle again, each picture, as it were, following along a groove made the deeper by repetition; each happier memory more bitter because of a subsequent knowledge of its transitoriness and issue; each painful memory the more painful because familiarity and habit of view cast light on the corners where the flame burned and the asps struck.

Suddenly her undisciplined emotions focused. From the phantasms of the past, and from her disordered dreams, a centre of supreme interest disclosed itself. What strange things had happened that had transformed her lover into a man crazed, and drove him from home? Was there something in connection with that strange old blind man and his night wanderings up to Warren Hill that had changed his life and hers?

She opened the door and looked out into the sultry night. The guns sounded more clearly, and the stars shone with a serene radiance. She glanced back to the child and caught up a cloak; then, picking up a pair of rough shoes in her hand, she ran swiftly down the footpath toward the Ridge track, her bare feet making no sound upon the grass. She had resolved to follow Billy Blind.

The Bear spread across the sky before her as she turned, and she ran straight towards the Pole Star, sometimes upon grass, and sometimes upon a harder surface. There was but one cottage beside her own so close to the summit of the Ridge, and it was dark and empty. Away to the right glimmered a light or two in Maldon, and once, at a great distance, she heard a bugle call. For nearly a mile she continued her way, and then the tall shapes of two windmills told her she was near the end of the Ridge. She turned eastwards, guiding herself by them, yet not going close enough to be seen by chance by the inhabitants.

And now she came close to Warren Hill, and the track failed her. Gorse and brier tore her legs and feet. She pulled on her shoes and clasped her cloak about her face. She travelled more slowly now, only vaguely sure of her direction, and staying to avoid trees and shrubs that impeded her.

Suddenly the trees ceased, and she knew that she was close to the old Camp. She hurried forward, and there, in the starlight, the scene of her dream re-enacted itself. Before her rose the walls of the great earthwork, broken by the path upon which she found herself. The ramparts curved away into darkness, and it was more by a consciousness than by visual sight that she realised the scene.

She stared towards the centre of the Camp with wild eyes, her heart beating quickly, for above the barrow rose a lambent light, and before it bent a solitary figure. Even as she dreamed, so she saw it. She looked round, expecting to see Jordan, and waiting for Billy Blind to turn, but the darkness behind her was impenetrable, and the old man did not change his position.

Step by step she approached, her courage upborne by a power seemingly not her own. With a sense of terror, she had the sensation of being attracted, as though her feet were obeying another will, there in the fire, or the barrow, or the man, she could not say which.

She was close, and her powers of endurance failed. She fell kneeling upon the bracken and waited. Somewhere at infinite distance, as though the impression transmitted to her senses had been heard by another, she knew that the sound of guns rolled and echoed; above, she was conscious of stars and night, but again it was to her not as an original sensation but as a fact told to her. The rampart and the barrow seemed to belong to unreality, and the man before her a figure in a dream that would tremble and vanish. Only the fire seemed real, and she bent her full attention to it.

It seemed to her to have shape and character, but of a quality utterly unearthly. She knew somehow it had risen from the barrow. It was of a white and pearly radiance that reminded her vaguely of moonlight, and it appeared to be upon a horizontal plane, like a table, and, as she thought, circular, with undefined edges that glowed more intensely. She surveyed it with a sort of desperation, marvelling at its beauty, and with a sort of belief that she was beyond all things that concerned her bodily and personal fate, and was arrived at her ultimate end. She felt an impulse toward union with this strange force, even though it should mean agony unspeakable.

As she looked at it, it changed. She discerned, as it were, within the fire, a red flame that was part of it and yet existed separately. It moved slowly, lengthening, shortening, changing. Presently another flame of similar character grew and moved within the plane. And these twin flames had not only an intense vitality, they had a mysterious personal essence. They glowed as they moved, with strange and varying pulsations, they suggested life and material existence sublimated.... Marabella gazed, rapt.

Presently she grew dazed. For some time past she had been able to see nothing but the luminous plane. The old man had passed out of her consciousness. Now she suddenly became aware of him in a troubled way. He was moving. Kneeling there, with her eyes closed to the intolerable radiance, with her hand clasping her hood to her throat, she turned vaguely to the man. He was aware of her, it seemed. Slowly he rose and moved towards her. The unearthly light illuminated both. He stood before her, and she

forced herself to look at him, in a sort of desperation.

She found herself gazing at an old face of singular beauty; ecstatic, questioning. The eyes were wide open and surveying her. Beyond all question they saw her. He was not blind now. He stood, a little old man, bowed and kindly, his face shaded by long, white locks, one hand grasping a staff, the other stretched to touch her shoulder. The light over the barrow waned.

"Thou hast seen?" he asked at length, and the sound of his voice came as something new to her. She had felt as though her senses had no more ways to serve her.

"Yea, sir," she answered, and could find no other word. The light died away and left them in the dark. There was a silence.

"I would know why God hath shown thee this mystery," the old man said at length. "Who art thou?"

"I am Marabella," she answered. Then defiantly, "they call me the Strange Woman in the village – and they call thee Billy Blind."

"I know it, child," said the old man. "Yet they err, for I see thee clearly now. In this place only, I see. Hither I come to be healed of my blindness; and perchance thou hast been led hither to be healed of thy – strangeness."

"Yonder Bale-fire, sir," she said fearfully; "what is it?"

He bowed himself in the darkness, as in prayer, for a while. The guns awoke again in the distance.

"Pray, child," he said at last. She shook her head hopelessly. He bent to her in a searching manner.

"Make the holy sign, then," he pursued: and her hand, lifeless, refused its office.

The man touched her head with his fingers, and a sudden newness came to her. Her hand moved of itself, almost before her will directed it, and made the sign of the Cross.

'Now, speak what is within thine heart." There seemed a rending and shattering of emotions and ways of thought that had grown with her during past years A little sob came from her.

"Lord, if thou wilt, thou canst make me clean." The words came from her without thought. She was convinced now that she was dreaming. These things happen not but in dreams.

There was silence again. The old man moved to the barrow and bowed over it. A faint luminosity arose from it and waned again. He returned to her.

"I will; be thou clean," he said. She knew he was making the sign over her. Somewhere in her consciousness she felt a vague revolt against what seemed blasphemy, but the sense of security and newness overcame it. She rose from her knees and went trembling towards the barrow. A young oak grew upon the top of it, and she leaned upon the tree, sitting there upon the ground, with her hood fallen back from her face. Her eyes sought the figure of the old man, standing there, leaning upon his staff.

"Tell me, sir, the mystery of this awesome place, and what is that light that waxeth and anon waneth."

Billy Blind pondered. "Why, if to the Magdalen, then to thee also... else wherefore art thou led hither? ... Listen, Marabella. Many years ago, amid those that defended this Stronghold against the Danes that came up the river was a certain chief that loved a woman with an exceeding great love. A Christian was he, and even such he made her, and they were wedded. But it befell that the Danes prevailed, and all fled from the Stronghold, save these two. She could not, and he was unwilling to leave her."

Marabella understood as by intuition. Her heart went out through the long past to the woman in woman's need.

"Yea, pity her... The Danes slew both, and they lie in the sepulchre here." The old man touched the barrow reverently with his staff. After a pause he went on.

"Now the mystery of the soul is this. We be more great than we do know; more than a store of memories won from the years, more than the sum of sorrows and sins and feeble victories that we do recount since our birth. The thing that is *I* and the thing that is *thou* do extend beyond what we deem to be self; a strange, undiscovered country – strange, yet nevertheless familiar."

"Yea, that I believe, sir, though I wist not others knew it, yet somehow I have known it. I, Marabella, am greater and more strangely wonderful than the Marabella others do know."

"Then hearken yet again. In the soul of each one of us there lies the Abyss. Now here in our waking life we be separate

34

beings, but in the Abyss one soul doth mingle with another in an intercommunion. It is not that identity is destroyed, but a sharing of being is made possible by the goodness of God... Canst understand, child?"

"Why, partly, sir. Doth not religion teach somewhat of that?"

"Yea; and now one supreme mystery. The Lord Christ doth use the Abyss in the soul as the way by the which He may come to us."

Marabella was silent. The man's voice thrilled with the intensity of his message. Doubt again swept over her. Was this dream, or waking? If this were real, was this man crazed? Her eyes went back to the barrow, and she thought of the two lying beneath. She put her hand to the turf, and to her fancy it seemed to heave slightly beneath her touch.

"Now it hath pleased God to make know to me the way of prayer," said Billy Blind. "And, moreover, the spiritual and real uplifting of mine own self, or downcoming of the divine Presence – in truth, there is no more or less one than the other – this hath He vouchsafed to make open and plain by a manifestation or epiphany that sense may perceive – even the appearance of a fire, like the body of heaven in its clearness...

"That which enfoldeth all, and lieth beneath all, that lighteth not only every man that cometh into the world, but also everything wherein is life that is not only the Word, or expression of the Originator, but also the End, and the Way whereby life cometh to it. This hast thou come more closely to, child, than many seers and seekers of the world. Thou sawest an epiphany of the Abyss the which Christ doth use for His work... Didst see aught in the table of light?"

"Yea, master, a division of flames, or a divided flame – I know not."

"The souls of the man and the woman I told thee of. By some design of the Lord of all, in the place where the bodies lie, there may their souls shine in the glory of the Abyss. And there may even thou and I come to a contemplation of them. Here, and here alone, mine eyesight is restored. By the light of the Abyss I saw thee and the hill with the great walls and dykes... I do think that though art brought hither by no chance. Wilt thou look upon it again? Thou mayst, if thou canst pray."

"I fear, master."

"And I also, child. But one there is that casteth out not only sin but fear."

Crouched upon the top of the barrow, Marabella covered her face. Her memory caught at an old text.

"Lord, I believe. Help thou mine unbelief!"

"According to thy faith, so be it to thee." The man had come close to the edge of the sepulchre and was bowed before it. There was silence. The sound of the guns in the distance had died away.

Chapter VI

THE DIVIDED FLAME

Marabella stared down at the shadowy turf, her head bowed, her hands clasped between her knees. She was in great fear, notwithstanding the consolation and encouragement of the old man. In fact, she was distraught with the contending qualities that had characterized her being within a short time. She remembered the man in the Gospels describing himself as Legion, and felt a similar multiplication of personality. She had an impulse to fly to a more familiar environment of scorn and sin and wild resentment; and then suddenly her desire passed with a wonderful completeness, leaving her expectant, hopeful.

Billy Blind spread out his hand over the mound, and as Marabella looked, lo, it seemed dark against the background of turf. With infinity slowness, and yet with a kind of insinuating sweetness, a pale mist emanated from below. It gathered a certain opacity, and faint suggestions of colour appeared. Then it suddenly disclosed an infinitude of depths. The luminosity increased, and it became less a plane of moonlight mist than a fire that gleamed with dancing and living lights within it, like an enormous opal.

Vague suggestions of nature occurred to Marabella's mind as she witnessed the miracle. Skies and constellations, that seemed not remote, but of an intimate life. Tumultuous seas and soft foam-touched wavelets that teemed with vitality and became, as it were, part of herself; a world of wings and tendrils and flowers; leaves and swinging foliage that seemed caught by winds; peaks of infinite remoteness; sunsets and dawns of unimaginable splendour, tracts of sand and vast spaces of unstained snow – these she knew and caught in symbols rather than saw their visible presentments, and then, with awe, she became aware of a presence that had the value of a human soul.

It was as a flame that she conceived it, yet it had a strange vitality and distinctiveness. It leaped and reddened, turning and playing among the multitudinous life, formless, spiritual, yet in some awe-inspiring way, human. She knew beyond all telling that it had qualities that sanctified its intense passion.

Its very energy was that of a conquering spirit. It had drawn upon the Abyss, and Marabella

remembered that it was the Abyss wherein the Master chose to make His presence known and His power felt. A longing from the original deeps of her own soul rose in her, and she bent close to the intense radiance. She caught a glimpse of the old man at her side. His eyes were wide and ecstatic, and he was looking at her. She had a sense of fragrance and of music…

The strange divided flame rose to her, and she closed her eyes. Her own soul seemed drawn from her, and passed an instant of agonizing purgation. Then her knowledge widened. Barriers of old habit of outlook and action were riven. Purposes, intuitions, things meaningless to her old self suddenly recalled themselves with an intense significance. The flame had given her a gift, the gift of revelation of herself, a greater self than she had every dreamed of. She had drawn, too, from the Abyss. She became conscious of a companion that was yet her own life…. Here she would cease, she thought. This was death, and the desirable life that lay beyond purging, fiery gates. This was the paradise that was the reward of whoever might endure the swinging of the sword of the seraph….

Something clouded her consciousness, and she felt as though travelling through endless space. She opened her eyes to darkness. She was kneeling by the tree on the top of the mound, and the desolation and emptiness of the night spread about her. Above, the stars glittered, and the Camp stood in its loneliness about her, its ramparts rolling away majestically into gloom, like immortal shapes amid the transitoriness of the seasons and the generations of humanity.

She looked for the old man, but he was nowhere to be seen. Slowly she arose and stared down at the sepulchre, but it remained dark and voiceless. She turned homeward. The sudden revulsion had swept her like a great wave, yet her fear was gone, and she knew that within her soul there was opened a gate, wherethrough a glory, a heroism, and a passion for righteousness and beauty flowed. The soul of the man whom untimely death had liberated that it might find in the Abyss the well of life, had given her of the bounty he had received from the fount whence the Master poured forth the riches of His own nature.

She went slowly homeward along the Ridge under the shadowy trees. The night air was soft; away to the east there was the faintest indication of dawn, and somewhere a bird called. When she came to the outhouse she paused; Abel was stirring and talking to himself. She felt a new pity for the poor creature, and thought of the contempt she had used towards him. She pushed the door of the cottage open gently, and went within. Her child moved and rose in the bed silently. She flung herself beside him, clasping him passionately, and broke into wild weeping. It was long years since she had wept.

Chapter VII

THE MISSION

The young man who had been newly ordained priest pursued his way toward Maldon. He was disguised as a pedlar, and bore a pack with him, finding it necessary at whiles to make some excuse for not trading. He did not enter the town, which was full of soldiers and had a singular air of activity, but kept to the western side of it, where he found an inn with a decayed signboard that had three lions upon it, being known as 'The Cats.' Here he tarried two or three days, each day going out carefully, somewhat before noon, and making his way to the vicinity of an ancient oak that overhung the road on the way to the town. The tree spread out some ten or twelve feet above the ground, and was dwarfed with many centuries of pollarding.

The young man would seat himself at the foot of the oak each day precisely at noon, and read a paper carefully. Then he would take out his Bible and read therein for an hour, after which he would rise and take his way elsewhere. He was a personable young man, with a fresh complexion and a rather puzzled expression. His mouth was habitually kept tightly shut, and his eyes had a way of taking in his surroundings at a glance. Folks at the inn rather distrusted him, and would not speak much before him. He was thought to be on some secret business, and indeed that was the truth.

On the third day upon which the young priest had taken up his position under the oak, a soldier appeared from the west, leading a horse that had evidently fallen lame. The soldier wore a breastplate somewhat dinted, and leathern garments with high riding-boots. A steel cap hung at the saddle, and upon the man's head was a broad-leaved hat. His dark hair was worn rather longer than the Parliament army was wont to wear it, and the clean-shaven face above the fallen linen collar was that of a scholar, being expressive of great earnestness and self-discipline. He looked pale and tired from walking far in riding-boots. He drew abreast of the young man beneath the oak, and wiped his face, removing his hat

as he did so. The reader desisted for a moment, and looked keenly at the soldier.

"What wares in the pack, master pedlar?"

"Truth, I am sold out; but what will you be lacking, sir?"

"Why, a sound horse to start withal, and a mind at ease to go on with!"

"The horse hath delayed you, sir?"

"Yea, two days. Find me a text in thy Bible to hearten me. I see thou art a religious pedlar."

There was an instant's pause, and the two looked at one another. With a casual turn of the leaves, the pedlar read out:

"Art thou he that should come, or do we look for another?"

The soldier signed with relief. He came and held out his hand.

"His name is John," he answered. "I am Simon Freeman, at your service. Thou art the man I was to meet, as I think?"

"Jordan Gyll, sir; a humble clerk in Holy Orders, and priest of but two days' standing. I have a letter for thee, and right glad I am to deliver it." He groped deeply in his doublet and produced a letter wound about with silk and sealed. Freeman glanced at the superscription.

"To the General, as I thought," he said. "'He is at Maldon?"

"Yea, but scarce any do know of it, though the place is full of soldiers. Some secret affair. What news of Colchester?"

"Like to fall any day. I pray God I be not too late through this beast! He lowered his voice. "This is from the Lady Margaret?"

"Ay; come to my hands through an old priest who helped ordain me and, as I think, from the bishop. I was told to wait thee here."

"I have been on her ladyship's affairs in England. At Harwich it was told me I was to come hither, and I had the password. Dost know of this matter?" Freeman tapped the letter.

'Only that it concerneth her brother nearly. In faith I would that I know no more. I have enough of secrets in these times. To have to use the Prayer Book secretly, and be ordained secretly, and minister secretly…. When will God lift the cloud from off the country?"

The soldier seemed indisposed to argue. He concealed the letter with care.

"Well, God keep you, reverend sir. We may meet again under other circumstances."

The two men looked at one another and clasped hands. For a moment an extraordinary significance appeared to be behind the words, and there was a certain solemnity about the silence.

"God bless you, Master Freeman, and give fortunate issue to the matter you have in hand!"

The soldier led off the lame horse in the sunshine toward Maldon, and the pedlar gathered up his pack, pocketed his Bible, and with a sigh of relief turned back to the inn. The mission entrusted to him by the bishop was a thing that preyed on his mind. He had feared he should fail to find the man, or be robbed, and he was thankful to have discharged his duty without difficulty, though with some delay. The heat of the August day forbade his quick walking, and as he went he had leisure to think upon a matter hitherto forced downward from his consciousness, but to be faced. He recounted the experience. He had gone back for his Bible to the ruined palace at Wickham Bishops, and he had turned back and had seen, unmistakably, the figure of the old man he had known as 'Billy Blind' issuing from the gate.

The past suddenly gripped him. The sweetness of a face; its dark beauty; the tenderness and desirableness of the girl, her provocativeness, the surrender of both to one another. And against that, the thing of diabolic import – the taunt of Marabella about the strange old man who journeyed up to Warren Hill, coming from God knows whence, and going for God knows what purpose. He had followed him that night and had realized what he had been told of by fearful village-folk with shuddering. He had beheld necromancy and wizardry. And within him there had been the clear and unmistakable conviction that Marabella and this wizard were at one to ensnare him, body and soul.... Billy Blind had turned and looked at him – the blind man had seen him, that he could swear – and there was invitation in the look.

He recalled the realization of his soul's peril with awe; the tales of magic; the quarrel with his mother about his love for Marabella; the bitter sweetness of his passion; the sudden revelation that he was on the edge of spiritual destruction. He remembered how he stood there, sweating in the darkness, with Billy Blind standing before a magic light, looking round at him. He remembered how he plunged downward with a sob, anywhere – anywhere, to find a way to penitence and the pardon of God.... Not to his mother. He could not tell her of this thing. And so he had journeyed wildly northward, and had fallen ill by the way. Taking shelter in a lonely house, where hospitable folk had taken pity on him, he had found that they were a little community, with several priests among them, bound by rules to daily services and the keeping of the fasts and festivals. He had offered himself as gardener and servant, growing their produce, cutting their wood, and bearing water from the well for their needs. At whiles he attended their services, and so, slowly, a love for their orderliness of worship grew in him, and the gentleness and lustration of a new feeling for religion possessed and healed him. In this way it came about that, after long thought and confession, he had offered himself for orders in the Church of England, then under so great a cloud; and after a year's unobtrusive ministry, the outset of his priesthood was to be called along this dubious

way, lighted only by the conviction that he was doing what he was bidden to do by his spiritual superior, and that there should come a time when the tyranny
should be overpast.

He now strode forward quickly through Danbury, passed Chelmsford, and came to Roxwell, where was the great house of Skreens. It was almost empty now, but an old steward received him quietly, having had information concerning him. He began to make himself known to those yet faithful to the Church of England in the neighbourhood.

In the meantime Simon Freeman had plodded wearily into Maldon. There was considerable activity in the town, and a subdued excitement was manifested in the streets, where groups of men, mostly armed, gathered and chatted. The doors of All Saints Church let in and out a number of people, and within the building different sermons were being preached in chancel and nave. An elderly and grave Presbyterian was preaching moderation and godly quietness, deprecating the use of force in the Lord's service, while an Independent excitedly called for the sharpening of God's sword to the extirpation of all Amalekites.

Freeman baited his horse at the Blue Boar and consulted his directions unobserved. He passed by Saint Peter's Church and struck down the steep hillside that marked the beginning of the Colchester road. At the doorway of a tall, white house on his left hand, he observed two soldiers standing on guard. They had their swords drawn and were fully armed, tall muscular men of the New Army, their faces weathered and set, their eyes glinting fiercely on all who ventured to stay and stare at them. These were curtly ordered away if they hesitated. They glared at Freeman as he approached, but he held his way towards them.

"I am on an errand to the Chief," he said quietly.

'Your warrant, master," answered one man, with obvious distrust.

Freeman, with much care, took out a purse and extracted a paper. The soldier took it and glanced at him. He stamped upon the brick floor. A clattering upon the stairs was followed by the appearance of another man. He was tall and thin and looked forbidding, clad in soiled black doublet and knee-breeches, with a crumpled linen collar about his scraggy throat. His grey hair stood up in stiff bristles and was cut very short. A worn leather belt was about his waist, and from it an inkhorn dangled. His thin, bearded face had an expression of displeasure as he looked at the messenger.

The soldier who had taken the paper passed it over to the newcomer without comment. The old man, with sharp glances, twirled it in his fingers, and with slow steps mounted the stairway again. There was a pause, and then quicker steps descended. A second man appeared, of a different type. He was almost fastidiously neat in his dress, though it was black. His linen at throat and wrists was spotless, and his shoe-buckles of silver. His eyes were bright and intelligent, though he lifted a long white hand to shield them from the light as he approached. His hair, parted in the middle, fell to his shoulders. Freeman uncovered to him, as by instinct.

"You have courage, friend, to press hither."

"I have good cause, sir."

"God prosper all good causes, Amen. Will you follow me?"

Simon Freeman followed Cromwell's secretary up the stairs. Upon the first floor were two more soldiers on guard outside a curtained door. At a sign from the secretary they opened it, and the two passed in. Freeman halted inside, while his conductor went forward.

A bulky man with a red and unprepossessing face looked steadily at the messenger from behind a table littered with books, parchments, a broad hat, an open Bible, a great sword, and a pair of horse-pistols. His hand rested upon a letter, gripping it. A half scowl came and went on his forehead. Simon Freeman saluted, knowing that he was in the presence of the man who had broken the power of the king.

"This is the man, sir, that beareth the message from Lady Margaret of Newcastle."

"Will you take it, master secretary?"

The secretary came to Freeman, who delivered the silken-wound paper he had received. Cromwell took it and turned it over without opening it.

"How came you, man, to find your way scathless to this very place? You must have good friends, or I am badly served."

"It is because one good turn doth deserve the like, sir. It may be within your memory that you did send to Oxford a messenger to the Duke of Newcastle. The man's life was endangered, and I had the good fortune to preserve it."

Cromwell showed interest. "I do remember," he said. "And I thank you for that service. So the debt hath been in some measure repaid by your safe passage hither. I will not ask how."

"I thank you, sir. I have none to accuse of treachery toward your person or your cause."

The General broke the seal and frowned over the letter. He read it carefully and handed it to the secretary, walking about the room in thought. The secretary read it with a perturbed face.

"Know you the import of this?" Cromwell asked suddenly of Freeman.

"Yea, sir. For if perchance I failed to deliver the letter, I was to give you the message by word of mouth. The Lady Margaret of Newcastle is certified that if Colchester fall, her brother, Sir Charles Lucas, will be executed. She prays you, therefore, to give me a letter to the General Fairfax that shall preserve his life."

"What think you, master secretary?"

"I do think it likely, sir, that it is intended. There was talk of his having broken parole, and thus being without the usage of war; yet have I gone into the affair, and he is clean. If he die 'twill be a matter of private vengeance, whereof I will appraise you."

"Yet surely, Fairfax…. It is the eleventh hour at Colchester, man. At any time the bells may ring and the beacon flare that shall tell of the fall thereof!"

Freeman groaned. "I do know it, sir. 'Tis pure mischance. I would give my life rather than miscarry!"

"Do you wait without… Master secretary!"

Freeman saluted and retired outside the door. He saw Cromwell plunge into earnest talk with his adviser. He waited impatiently for some minutes, coolly surveyed by the guards. Finally the door opened and the secretary appeared. He bore two letters in his hand, and these he gave to the messenger.

"The letter you require, sir, and God speed you for our honour as well as yours…. This other message take you to the Blue Boar, and ask for the cornet of Colonel Harlackenden's horse, who leaves for Colchester within an hour with a small body. You shall be preserved in their company, and find your way more readily to the General his presence. Farewell…"

He gave Freeman a peculiarly winning smile, and retired.

Chapter VIII

MISADVENTURE

Evening had fallen ere Freeman found himself well mounted and issuing from the Blue Boar at the tail of a small body of Colonel Harlackenden's cavalry, on the road for Colchester. He was consumed with impatience, but deemed it best to take advantage of the means offered to get to the besieged town, rather than chance going alone and being shot for a spy ere he won through to the presence of General Fairfax. The day had been hot, and the little troop jingled and sweated and creaked as they began the descent of the hill. His companions were typical men of the 'New Model,' most of them pious, but hard-bitten men, whose very narrowness and self-restraint lent a greater impetus to the affair they were committed to than would either sympathy or knowledge or idealism. Royalists, Presbyterians, Anabaptists, Papists, all seemed to them equally comparable to the heathen hordes destroyed by Israel on their entry into the Promised Land. Freeman listened to their talk, and decided to take no part in it. As the leader of the troop was informed, he was on a mission to Fairfax, and that procured him consideration.

At the foot of the hill there was a cry from behind. A man was throwing up his arms to stay them. The troop was halted, and the leader beckoned the man to approach. He was in attendance upon an officer of some consequence, who was waiting under an archway on the hillside, having just arrived, as was apparent from the condition of his horse. The leader of Harlackenden's horse climbed with some displeasure to the man who had called, and then approached the officer under the archway with deference. An animated conversation ensued, concluded only by the stranger giving a curt order, and turning away.

The upshot of the affair was that the orders to go straight along the main road to Colchester were cancelled. The men were to go to Chelmsford and join forces with another troop to escort munitions. Many were the complaints evoked by this new command. It meant taking two sides of a triangle instead of one to reach the apex. Freeman swiftly calculated chances, thinking of flight. He resolved, on the whole, it were better to adhere to the troop-commander to whom he had been committed. The probabilities were that he would not get through the leaguer otherwise.

With some sullenness the troop mounted the hill again and turned along the Danbury road. Ahead of them the sun was setting royally, and the brown foliage on either side of the way told of the passing of the year into autumn. A cloud-bank rolled up and blotted out the sunset, and the night promised to be dark.

They passed Saint Giles' Chapel, Woodham Mortimer church, the ancient oak, then Runsell, and in darkness climbed the flank of the Ridge that stretched away northwards. They came to a part of the road over which trees hung. A narrow chase turned off between large elms, and as the troop passed there came the sound of a call from the mirk.

"For the King!" cried a voice, and simultaneously there was a blaze of a firearm and an explosion. In a moment the troopers had ridden to the spot with their swords drawn, discharging their pistols in the direction from which the voice came. They found nothing, and re-formed in the darkness, trotting quickly on to Danbury.

Freeman took no part in the search for the ambush. His horse was trembling oddly. He put down his hand to soothe him, and found him in a dreadful lather of sweat. He was by now alone on the road, and determined to dismount. Suddenly the horse dropped under him and rolled on him. He had a moment's agony, and then unconsciousness took him.

* * * * *

A hammering in his temples was his first perplexing
sensation, and then a sharp paid in his thigh. He was lying by
the roadside in the quiet of the night. Stars were over him,
seeming remote and unconcerned. Against him his horse lay
dead. His own foot was tangled there somewhere, and an effort
to move agonised him almost unbearably. The troop had
evidently gone on without missing his presence among them.
He found that it was the horse's head that lay heavy on his
foot. With an effort that cost him great pain, he withdrew it. It
was evident that his leg was broken above the ankle. He felt
blood on his head too, and a sharp, pain from one of his ribs.

Instinct or some sense of smell of which he was unaware
told him that water was not far away, and he summoned up his
remaining strength to try and find it. He rose to hands and
knees and crawled, keeping his broken foot off the ground as
much as possible. Presently it jarred, and he stopped, sickening
with the pain. He was on grass now, and did not know where
the road was. He thought grimly of the irony of the thing. He
had been disabled by some royalist adherent – he, the sole
royalist in all the troop – he who was on a royalist mission!

He stopped, and a new distress took hold of him at that
thought. The mission would go unfulfilled, the letter
undelivered. Sir Charles Lucas would die for want of the paper
in his pocket that alone could save him. He groaned and
cursed his impotence, and then dragged on further. A little
moon emerged daintily from the filmy cloudlets, and, not a
dozen yards away, he saw water. He now remembered passing
the pond at the four-want way. There were some cottages
near, he knew, but he could not see them, nor determine their
direction.

He reached the pond, and revived himself by pouring water
over his head and face, drinking deeply afterwards. Then,
seated by the margin, he laved his broken foot, and, taking his

sword from his side, he bound it against instep and knee with his belt, to keep it in some sort of position. The pain and effort of this exhausted him for a while; then he drew upon his resources of will, and crawled on again. The north star hung before him now, and he determined to make for that. All points were alike to him, and as he knew not where the houses might be, he thought he might as well aim at the star as anything else. He went on mechanically, pausing at intervals. At times he would find himself fronted by unsurmountable briers and gorse. Then he would patiently work round the obstacle, and look for his star again. He began to feel light-headed, but made himself go on, telling himself to continue at all costs, and setting his teeth. His fancy brought forgotten faces before him; his father with his stern, religious discipline, his devotion to the king's cause as that of the anointed of the Lord. He remembered his schoolmaster, with his Spartan ideas of duty and self-control; his own determination to find life's meaning and worth in the service of a failing cause; the one hope - as he thought - of the realm, lying in the triumph of church and king. He remembered the face of one whom he could have loved, a bright, sweet face with a touch of roguishness and invitation to him, framed in the prim Puritan cap; of how he had gone apart and wrestled with his own longing, and conquered it for the sake of the work to which he had set his hand. He remembered isolated incidents in battles – his white uniform at the breach of the town wall at Hull, with the Duke of Newcastle urging them on; the failures, the varied missions and secrecies in which he had been engaged and had not failed in; a house in Stepney where these things were planned. And now it seemed that this was the end. He would find death prematurely, like so many better than himself. He wondered if death would give him vision, and of what or whom. Christ perhaps, or the saints; or his dead mother and father. At any rate the pain would stop then, and the stars would stop going round in circles....

Something dark loomed up before him. It was a door, and he scrabbled at it, and called in a voice that seemed not to belong to him. It opened, and a half-light showed him a beautiful woman standing with a child in her arms.

From the mire and dust where he grovelled upon hands and knees, he stared up wonderingly, and lifted up one hand in supplication.

"Jesu, mercy," he whispered; "Mary, help."

BOOK THE SECOND: TRYST

Chapter IX

TROUBLING OF THE WATERS

The feverish fantasies that whirled through Simon Freeman's mind, as he lay deprived of his ordinary faculties, had largely a religious element in them, produced by the impulse of his last conscious impressions. Spent and exhausted, he had dragged himself in the darkness to Marabella's cottage. He had believed death to be near, and with the idea of death were associated certain religious conceptions. His failing powers had taken in a vision, as he thought, of the Madonna and her divine Child, glimmering out of the darkness, and offering him, as it were, a first sight of spiritual realities.

Lying unconscious there, a broken man, wounded, and in dire need, he had been the object of patient care on the part of the girl. She had bound up his head and, shuddering at the task, had set the broken ankle as well as she might. Then she had roused Abel, greatly wondering, and together they had lain the man upon the only bed in the cottage. Through the night, Marabella had shared the child's pallet in the corner, scarcely sleeping, rising at times to put water to Freeman's lips, or to replace the bandage which he displaced in his feverish movements.

Towards morning he became quieter, and she slept a little, to wake later with a queer incursion of memory concerning the strange advent of the night before. She looked across to the bed, to discover the man's eyes open and gazing at her perplexity. She rose and carried water to him, which he drank with eagerness. He continued, however, to look questioningly at her. His face was startlingly pale and drawn, and his expression was almost that of a visionary. She stood with the early sunshine about her rich beauty, her arms, neck, and feet bare, her mass of dark hair falling about her lustrous eyes, and brilliant lips and cheeks. He tried to make recent experience a connected and coherent thing, and failed. A troubled sense of weakness overcame him as his memory broke down before the task he imposed upon it.

She gave him more water and moistened his forehead.

"Art better?" she asked, and he sighed as he heard her voice.

"Yea," he answered; 'I live.... Where is this?"

"Hard by Danbury," she said. "Mayst see the church spire through the window when thou art well. Sleep now."

"Who art thou?" said the man.

"Have patience and sleep. Art sorely hurt."

He closed his eyes again in a tired way and slept quietly. Marabella knelt and looked at him. From the deeps of her nature rose an overmastering joy that was new to her – the joy of service. This helpless being had been sent to her by God to pour out her new gift upon. She thought back for a swift moment of how she would have regarded formerly a stray and wounded soldier at her door; but now...

She moved about with a passionate exultation of soul, her footsteps noiseless, wetting bandages, touching with light and cleansing fingers the clotted and stained hair, the improvised splint, the twisted and sprained arm; darkening the window towards which the white face turned, hushing the child when he awoke, and Abel when he stumbled about, bearing water or splitting wood close to the door.

She moved about, crooning a tuneless music. This, then, was some grace vouchsafed to her, some emanation from the Abyss that had dowered her soul with a new and divine character. She could pray now, she thought, and the idea linked itself immediately with the child. She went over to him, busy with his breakfast of goat's milk and coarse bread. The

54

child's eyes shone through the thick thatch of hair wonderingly as she put her hands together. She knelt and closed her eyes.

'Water!" The man waked and needed her. She rose and went over to him, and he drank, looking at her. Sighing, he tried to move and felt the quick pain. Sweat stood on his forehead, and she opened the door and let in the late summer air that blew cold over the hill.

"How came I thus, lady?"

"Wilt thou not rest? Thy head will ache if thou talk."

"Nay, 'tis better; but I cannot remember.... Stay, my horse was shot.... I was riding.... Didst find me by the road?"

"Thou didst come to my door in sore straits, and must needs abide. Be at peace; they will not shoot thee here."

"Who art thou?"

A moment of panic seized her. Her old self still held her. Should she deny her past? It was becoming an untrue thing to her. And then the supreme need of sincerity filled her. She must not smirch her new life at the very outset.

"I am Marabella," she said tremulously.

"Marabella – what else?" he asked, and there seemed a relentlessness about the question.

"Nought else," she answered. "I have none other name."

The wounded man looked puzzled. The red blood ran up her neck and flooded her face. He saw it, and seemed to be searching in his mind for a reason.

'None other name? What do folk call thee then?" he asked simply.

She clasped her hands and bent towards him. A sob rose in her throat.

"They call me 'Marabella – the Strange Woman,'" she broke out in a sort of flaming defiance, and turned away, her shoulders heaving with a wild emotion.

There was silence. The man's eyes searched the room as though looking for something. She turned instinctively and went to the corner of the room where the child was, catching him up in her arms. She kissed him passionately with tear-stained face, and her eyes burned at the man on the bed.

"Yea, he is mine," she broke out tumultuously; "and I am neither maid nor wife.... I am Marabella, the Strange Woman!"

She sank down in her familiar attitude, resting against the door, and staring out into the sunshine, weeping quietly. The man looked at her and thought, slowly and with difficulty.

He had had a strange upbringing of idealistic loyalty that required Spartan restraint and a self-discipline more than monastic. Both by temperament and by rigorous education he had had enforced upon him a withdrawal from worldliness and allurements of the senses. He had been taught to train thought and act to an extraordinary level of self-sufficiency, a shrinking sensitiveness to evil that had for compensation an iron devotion to the training of body and brain. Singled out by this combination of the qualities of soldierliness and asceticism, he had been the personal attendant of the Duke of Newcastle, and his trusted emissary in many matters. His clear and cold view of the duty that was to be done, despite discomfort or death, was the result of long and painful effort, and his character and story presented a peculiar distillation of chivalry and self-abnegation that had rendered him a man utterly lonely, yet finding nothing strange in the fact, nothing to cause complaint or suspicion. He moved amid a world of folly, passion and self-seeking, of greed and ambition, as in a place alien to him, like an armed knight making his way toward the dragon he was to slay, heedless of the roses that he crushed with his mailed heel as he went. Some new, disturbing emotion touched him now. He could not think nor judge, but his instinct spoke for him. He closed his eyes again.

"Do not weep, lady," he said. 'To me thou art as a ministering angel of God."

She became rigid and her sobs ceased. She set the child down; with parted lips, cheeks aflame, and eyes like lamps, she came towards him slowly.

It seemed that he was asleep once more.

Chapter X

MARABELLA RIDES

Simon Freeman awoke soon after dawn with a vague sense of trouble. During his sleep his memory had been unconsciously recuperating, and his dreams had more suggestions and reiterated impressions of real happenings than before. In the grey light he set himself to a sort of patient receptivity, allowing his memory to feel gently backward at its own pace into the recent past.

Then he stretched his arms painfully. They were clad in a strangely coloured garment that wrapped his body about above his shirt. It was apparently a faded robe that was threadbare yet clean, and had belonged to a woman. An edging of tarnished silver lace, the broken holes for points, the unstitched and frayed remains of rosettes – these he looked at quietly and curiously. He moved one leg beneath the rough blanket of bays; the other was fast set.

With difficulty he lifted his head and examined the room. In the farther corner was a broken screen covered with a leather cloth. He knew from the sound of regular breathing that Marabella and the child slept behind it, and he could see the end of the pallet upon the floor. A foot - small and brown and shapely - appeared, and he looked at it with strange interest.

His thought began to reconstruct Marabella. He owed his life to her, it would appear. She had succoured and tended him. His great riding-boots stood by the wall, and she must have removed them and, with what difficulty, had placed him upon the bed. His hat and sword and the remainder of his clothes lay near, showing evidence of his desperate struggle to save his life and win to safety.

He deliberately refused to force his mind to an attempt to reconstruct the circumstances that led to his plight. He knew that he had been in evil case, and this woman had succoured him. By and by, he told himself, he would remember what he had been doing.

He took in patiently other impressions – a rough table with earthenware upon it, the black, open fireplace with ashes just smouldering, an iron hook that came down the chimney, a staff, a pair of woman's shoes, a cloak, a horn lantern, a child's toy in the shape of a wooden ship. He closed his eyes again. Various sounds began within the house and outside. In the lean-to near by there was a subdued, incoherent murmur as of one talking in his sleep. A gander called loudly not far away, and cocks at different distances challenged one another.

And then arose a new sound that seemed full of premonition and suggestive of disaster. Away in the distance a deep, throbbing noise broke the quietness. The hut seemed to tremble slightly, and the sound waxed and waned, and was punctuated by louder single detonations.

Freeman realised what it meant with a sudden horror. It brought back in a flash the events that led up to his misadventure. It recalled his disastrous failure. The guns besieging Colchester meant that he himself should have been there by now, and his letter delivered to Fairfax. And he was lying here, the letter in his breast pocket. He endured acute distress. A man's life was at stake, and his own honour, and his character for never having failed a trust. He put his hand to his forehead and wiped sweat from it. He turned his face upon his coarse pillow, and tears fell from his eyes.

A light of resolve came to him. Somewhere a horse must be found. Somehow he could make his way. Life would hold out till then. It must be God's will that this should not fail.

He raised himself in bed, and set the sound foot to the floor of beaten earth. His head swam, and he waited till the faintness should pass. Then, with great care, he lifted his broken foot, set in splints of homely sort, and put it by the side of the other. His face was contorted with pain, but he reached out, edging himself along the bed to the pile of his garments. He had just clutched them when nature gave way. He fainted and fell upon the ground, a pathetic figure of broken manhood beneath a faded and gaudy robe, his hair matted and tangled about his white face.

Marabella awoke with the sound of the fall, and stared over the screen at the fallen man. Swiftly she rose and came to him as he lay, his clothing still fast clutched in his hand. She ran and shook Abel, who followed her silently, but in lively fear. The boy had slept in the clothes he had worn by day, but was without covering to his legs, and his witless face looked more than ever without intelligence, and overcast by the effect of heavy sleep. He regarded the wounded man with dislike and ill-favour. He had a dull emotion of jealousy strong within him, and it was only by sheer dominance that Marabella obtained his help. Together they lifted the man to the bed and covered him. The girl bathed his face.

'Go, Abel," she said, and the lad went, muttering to himself.

Freeman soon recovered, and stared at Marabella with despair in his eyes.

"So you would leave me," she said. "I do not marvel at that, but at the folly to try yet awhile."

He said nothing, and she went about setting things to rights, her feelings strangling her utterance. She felt bitter, yet in a strange way, glad to suffer. He knew she misunderstood him, but the greatness of his failure overshadowed consideration for her trouble. He pictured the surrender of the town, the entry, the ceasing of the guns, the mock trial and condemnation of the leader, the grief of the Lady Margaret who was loyalty incarnate, and who expected the like steadfastness from him. He beat impotently upon the robe that covered him and gave a loud sob. Marabella stopped and looked at him.

"Nay, surely there is more the matter than my company," said she. "I have little right to ask thee, but the right of gratitude for some small aid rendered…. I say it but to offer to add thereto, if it please you," she went on proudly.

"You may command my life, lady," he groaned; "but there is far more than my life's worth in this matter!"

She came and sat by the hearth, placing small twigs in the hot ashes and blowing upon them till they blazed. He watched her movements, her thin fingers, her curved lips, scarce conscious of them, yet compelled. Then he began to tell her, haltingly, of his name, his mission, of the letter to General Fairfax in his doublet, and of what hung upon it. And as he spoke the guns ceased to fire.

She sat wide-eyed, her hands round her knees, listening to him.

"So then," she said at length, "some trusty person must needs deliver that letter to the General, ere the town be taken, to save Sir Charles Lucas his life…." She looked round helplessly. "I know none who would go," she said, "save Abel… and yet 'tis not far – twenty miles… Why…"

She stood staring at the heap of Freeman's clothes – the hat, the sword, the long boots.

"Myself will do it!" she cried. "Thou canst be left for a day and a night if need be…. I will put bread and water and pulse, and thou and the child will do well." She stamped her bare foot with determination.

A gleam of hope came to Freeman's face, and died away again.

"Nay, 'tis folly," he said."'Twould not by possible for thee to win through the lines and find thy way, unmolested, to Fairfax…. This Abel, now – could he not find one to go? I would give money."

She bent swiftly and caught up the clothes in her arms. A look of joy came into her face. She ran from the room and climbed a ladder that led to a tiny loft. Presently she descended slowly, and Freeman marvelled at her. The boots were too large, and the thick jerkin, folded and belted, encumbered her movements. The leathern breeches sagged grotesquely, and the sword trailed noisily. The sleeves were folded back from her slim wrists, and the scarf was set about her shoulder as no man would set it, yet in her face and bearing was a fierce determination that outweighed the short-comings of her apparel. She held the letter up.

"I will win through with it," she cried, "and thou shalt not be shamed. Surely God sent thee hither for this!"

Freeman murmured protesting words, to which she would not listen.

"Abel," she cried, stamping her big boot. The door opened, and the shambling form of her half-brother appeared. He gaped at her speechlessly.

"A handful of hay and a halter!" she said: "and go thou and catch the white horse by the pond.... The Lord hath need of him.... Bring him hither. Nay, no questions.... Swiftly!"

She cast a cloak about her, and put together some food-scraps, tying them in a bundle and securing the knot with her strong, white teeth.

"For God His sake, lady, hither and let me tighten thy sword. Did ever weapon hang so? And the scarf... 'Ware those spurs, moreover. ... Ah, now."

She came to him to be set right, stooping down. As she did so her hair fell forward. He gave a little gasp.

"I should have thought of it," she said. "Wait, and you shall see."

She made for the wooden hutch, and drawing from it a pair of shears, cut her hair straight across at her chin's level. The dark locks fell upon the floor in a dusky heap, and she looked at them rather ruefully. Then she moved them with her foot till they were hidden beneath the bed. She set the hat upon her head and secured it.

"Now, tell me what must be done. Where lies this General Fairfax?"

"At Lexdon, lady, on the high road this side of Colchester, if thou win so far. There is a battery of great guns there, so I hear, and hard by is the headquarters of the General. Take this ring, if thou'rt let by any, and show it. Demand instant audience of the General, and say thou hast advices from General Cromwell. But I misdoubt me sorely. Thou wilt take the boy? He may be of help."

"Ay, I did think so. He will be obedient at the least. May win through if I fail.... May bring thee news."

The sound of hooves has heard. Abel sat astride a strong, white horse with a halter about his neck. The boy and the horse evidently knew one another, for the guiding had been accomplished by pulls and thwacks. An ancient bridle was hunted up from the hutch and put upon the animal, and a hop-sack was thrown across his back and secured. Abel wound the cloak about himself. He might have been dumb for all he spoke. He merely obeyed and gaped.

Marabella went and looked at her sleeping child, and then mounted by the aid of a stool, while Abel sat pillion behind her, clasping her belt. His bare legs stuck out queerly, and the sword dangled against them. Marabella pulled her hat down and bent forward. She turned back carelessly and patted the leather jerkin over the pocket where was Cromwell's letter. Freeman had craned his neck to look from the window, and she saw his face, startlingly white, framed by the ivy-grown sash. She cried a farewell and turned to go.

Suddenly she reigned in the horse and rode him past the door, peering in. She called out directions as to her child's food. She had seen, however, what he had thought to see. Freeman was groping beneath the bed for the locks of severed hair. She coloured and frowned, and set spurs to the white horse, who trotted briskly towards Hatfield with his double load.

Chapter XI

THE ATTEMPT

There was no deep water at the ford dividing the parishes of Little Baddow and Hatfield Peverel, except where the great mill-wheel turned and thrashed slowly in the current, the stream spreading widely over the meadows. Abel dismounted and waded, leading the horse that seemed to know instinctively where the footing was sure. Mist clothed the countryside thickly, and gave promise of heat. They walked the horse up the hill, and the girl took opportunity to try and provide against misadventure through Abel's ignorance.

"Wilt ever do as I tell thee, Abel?"

Abel looked at her, dog-like and intent. "Ay, sister," he said.

"We ride to Colchester, where there are soldiers fighting."

"They do use great guns, that keep I wakeful a' nights." He looked uneasy.

"Yea, but the guns will not fire at we... Hearken; I have a letter in my pocket. See.... It must go to General Fairfax. Say that after me."

"A letter for Fairfox... What sort o' fox by that? Taketh geese belike."

"Nay – a man, a soldier. If harm befall me, take thou the letter and find him.... Fairfax, at Lexden."

"What harm, Marabella?"

"Nay, I know not. But see, a man's life doth hang on thee and me. The letter must go!"

Abel pondered, and then straightened himself up. "A shall see the soldiers."

"Yea, and they shall try to make thee afeared with their shouting and their great guns, maybe. But thou and I will not be afeared for them. Shall us?"

"Nay, sister; thou hast a sword, and I my knife…. Yon man with the broke leg. Who is he?"

"Master Freeman, sent by God with the letter. We must needs take it, for he cannot. We do take God His letter now, Abel. Wilt mount again?"

He climbed up, and they struck into the high road, trotting along under the elms. They passed Witham ere the place was awake, save that at the "White Hart" there were soldiers lying at rest under the archway, dust-covered. They jeered at the strange pair, who took no notice of them. At Kelvedon they met a body of cavalry, with shining breastplates and steel caps, coming towards them. They were singing some hymn in deep tones. A man in the hedge called out to the party: "Be Colchester wall down yet?"

"All but, lad. They need us not now. The sword of the Lord hath struck for us. The malignants do ask for terms of surrender again…. Hold up, boy! Art crazed?"

Marabella, hearing the talk as she cantered past, had struck the horse to urge him to go faster, and there had nearly been a collision. The cavalry moved past her in a cloud of dust, the men looking curiously at her as she rode, the sweat pouring down her face, and Abel sorely preoccupied in keeping his seat. He sniffed, and tried to make the chafing seat more comfortable. The sword banged and clattered against his bare legs.

At Marks Tey the horse was evidently wearying. Abel dismounted and ran by the side, holding to the bridle. They had not heard the guns since their start, and Marabella was silent, her mind filled with forebodings.

When they reached Stanway they entered the dismantled church for a few minutes' rest. A fierce-looking and bearded man, with a steeple-hat set upon his head, surveyed them. He was in hot controversy with a small, round-faced, leather-clad man that had a singular tuft of hair upon his chin. His head was bare, and he had an open Bible in his hand, which he was beating to emphasize his arguments. Seeing Marabella, he called on her to remove her hat, which she had forgotten to do. His opponent cried to her to keep it on. Fearful of being involved in the quarrel, the two went out of the building, and flung themselves beneath a tree. They closed their eyes to rest them from the dust and glare. Scarcely had the girl done this that she began to dream. A touch on the arm awakened her.

A young soldier was standing by her, at whom Abel was staring in some alarm. A steel cap was upon his head, and a bright corselet covered his leather jerkin. His legs were clad in leathern breeches, with high boots reaching nearly to his waist; a sword hung from his scarlet sash, and round his neck was dangling a silver cornet. A few yards away a young lady sat upon a roam horse. She wore a broad hat with a sweeping feather, a falling lace collar, and a riding-dress of grey. Her fair curls were ranged in a row upon her forehead, and her eyes were blue and childish. She was holding the horse of the young officer
by the bridle.

Abel got slowly to his feet, and Marabella followed him. The soldier's eyes travelled rapidly over her clothing, and the girl felt her face flush. She pulled her hat down farther, and stared back with an assumed carelessness.

"Who are ye?" said the officer.

"Sir, I have a message that presseth. I have come hot-foot, and I wearied by the way.... Abel, the horse!"

"Nay, boy: stay there. Did ye ride together"

"Aye, master," said Abel; 'save when I ran; and my feet be sore." He came forward and stared at the cornet with an intense interest that overcame his awe. The officer held out his hand to Marabella.

"Your sword, boy." He frowned with the exaggerated authority of a youth not yet used to command, and the girl drew the weapon clumsily from the scabbard. The officer took it and examined it with care.

"I think ye lie," he said. "Ye are royalist. What do ye so near our lines? Answer truth, or I have ye shot!"

"I lie not. I have a message for General Fairfax. If you will bring me to him, you will see." Marabella felt her breast heaving. She clenched her hands and felt her courage ebb. She felt wretchedly weary, and her head ached painfully.

"What is this message, boy?"

"'Tis for General Fairfax. I give it only to him."

The young man paused, and the lady on horseback drew near. She looked curiously at Marabella.

"Well, Robert?"

"A spy, as I do think, or refugee from Colchester. Stand thou, and let the horse be fetched."

He turned to mount his own horse. In a flash Marabella had taken the letter from her breast and had passed it to Abel.

"Go," she whispered. "As I told thee!"

The lady on the roam horse noticed the curious bending gesture of the shoulders Marabella made as she reached for the letter. Her face lighted up with a smile. She watched Abel shambling after the wearied horse. Marabella remained standing listlessly, apparently awaiting orders.

The young officer, now mounted, indicated that she should walk ahead of him up the high road towards Lexden. She obeyed, her big boots paining her. She was waiting in desperate anxiety to hear what Abel was doing, but dare not look round, lest her eagerness should be noticed.

"Follow, lad," called the officer, and he rode behind Marabella side by side with the lady. The procession went slowly up the road. To the girl's distress, Abel was coming after them on the white horse. So it seemed he had not understood.

Suddenly there was a wild clattering behind. The officer turned with a suppressed curse. Abel was in full flight, his bare legs and arms clinging to the horse, his hair and cloak streaming. The officer was in a dilemma. Either he must leave his prisoner with his escort, or he must lose this flying tatterdemalion. He drew his pistol and fired, without further effect than to make the white horse gallop the faster and forget his weariness.

The explosion made the roam restless. The officer leaped from his saddle and seized Marabella roughly. He tore the scarf from her shoulder and with it bound her arms behind her. Her eyes burned at the indignity, but she said nothing. Her wrists were then made secure by a thong to the officer's stirrup. They proceeded up the road slowly, saying little.

Presently they came to an encampment that was being rapidly broken up. Tents were falling, and guns were being dragged by the excited soldiers. Bugles blew, and hymns rose upon the air. A body of horsemen swept down upon them.

"'Tis Colonel Harlackenden, cousin."

"Ay; now shall I be scolded."

The cavalry was halted in a cloud of dust, with much jingling and rattling. The leader, red and perspiring, drew near and saluted.

"At last, Alice. Come swiftly, we are belated. The soldier's a fool that lets himself be trammelled with a wife! Get to the house and make ready. We enter Colchester straightway. Thou must follow to the 'Red Lion' and seek me there.... Why, Robert, who is this?"

"A spy, as I think, sir. Hath some tale of a message for the General."

"More like some camp-follower, that hath stolen some soldier's raiment.... I may not stay.... Lock him up and search him. And if you think well, shoot him. And follow on to the town. Your brother, Alice, is here with his men, and the more part of our army is within the gates. The malignants have surrendered to mercy." He raised his sword, and the hard-faced men behind him began a hymn. Mistress Harlackenden waved her hand as the cavalry jingled and clattered on. Then she urged her horse to the side of the prisoner.

"Give me leave to speak with the spy, Robert."

"Why, certes, cousin. Wouldst though give ghostly counsel ere he die, for die methinks he shall. Who knoweth but that he would slay the General? There are such desperate fellows about."

"I do think this one not desperate. I would speak along with him."

Cornet Robert Mildmay looked at her in surprise.

"What whim is this, cousin? Why, no, thou art in my care. He might attack thee and try to escape."

"Well, keep him bound, only go apart."

The young man deliberately loaded his pistol. Then he untied the thong that fastened Marabella's wrists to his stirrup.

"If thou try any crookedness, fellow, I shoot thee dead." And he rode his horse away a dozen paces, and sat with pistol ready.

Mistress Alice Harlackenden bent to Marabella. Her fair curls fell over her face, and her big feather shadowed it. Marabella lifted her dark eyes, and knew that her secret was read.

"Thou art a woman," said Mistress Harlackenden. "And thou wilt tell me what thou dost, dressed thus in a man's clothing."

Marabella's head dropped. "I have told truth, lady," she said. "I did bear a letter to the General to save a man's life. I bore it for one that could not come himself, being sore wounded.... And I thought best to make my way thus."

"I do believe thee. Where is the letter? If thou trust me, I will see it delivered, on mine honour."

"The boy that 'scaped hath it.... And oh, lady, I would not die for my child his sake!" And the tears made channels through the dust upon Marabella's face.

"Thy child? God's mercy!.... Nay, no more now. I will see thee again."

Cornet Mildmay rode up authoritatively. "If thou hast done, cousin," he said.

They continued their march silently. Presently they came to a long, gabled house, beneath great elms that overlooked the road. Here they dismounted, a soldier took the horses, and the prisoner was thrust into a cellar. Bread and water were given her, and her hands were loosed. Then the door was double-locked upon her.

Chapter XII

TIDINGS

Simon Freeman lay listening for the guns, and heard them not. He saw the grey light change to gold and a red streak smite on the wall of the cottage, moving slowly downwards. A beam entered the room, populous with dancing motes. He watched them gyrate, and thought it impossible that they should not be living things disporting themselves. Through the window he could catch sight of an elm tree, dull green, with a patch of early gold high up on one side. A carrion crow perched there for a little while, croaking horribly, then flew off towards Colchester....

The wheel of thought revolved in the man's head. His earlier years, coloured by an individual stubbornness of rectitude that made him so true a loyalist when the crisis came; his campaigns, at Hull and York with the Duke of Newcastle; his interview with the Lady Margaret, and his resolve to be worthy of the mission, if it cost his life; the secret methods necessitated by the times; the jeopardy of the man yonder in the besieged town; his own success with Cromwell, and now this bitter failure. He moved his leg in his trouble, and the physical pang, compared with the pain in his mind, was almost a relief. He thought of the grotesque couple on the white horse bearing the last chance of success. The lad, well nigh
an imbecile, and Marabella, the "Strange Woman," as she styled herself.... And the name was not inapt, could he but set aside the shameful implication. He would not dwell upon that. There was a story he had not heard. But, indeed, she was 'strange.' Hard and defiant in one of her numerous moods, tender and maternal in another; brave and selfless in another. And withal beautiful, with a dark, rich, southern beauty, mingled white and brown and black and deep red, and a glint

of fire. The impressions came across his consciousness like notes of music; he did not think upon her separate features of eyes and lips and hair. And the childish way she had of settling herself upon the floor, with an abandonment of lissom grace, and limbs that drooped in long lines....

He checked himself from thinking too disturbingly of her, and took in the contents of the room once more. Where was she now? Kelvedon? Feering? How had the horse taken the ford? He pictured the loungers at the inns calling out to the riders, the soldiers on the road that might stop her....

He heard a movement behind the rough screen, and then a sigh. It was evident that the child was waking.

"Robin," he called softly.

The child emerged, flushed with sleep, his fair hair over his eyes, his fingers thrust into his mouth. He stood up rather shakily, a beautiful creature, clad in a little night-shift that came scarce below his waist, his sturdy, bare legs and feet wide apart to steady himself. He looked at the injured man doubtfully.

"Mammy," he said at length.

Freeman talked soothingly to him, feeling un-practiced in the matter. He said that mother would come, and that they must have food in the meantime. He reached for the pannikin and soaked bread in the goat's milk, setting it by the side of the bed. Gradually confidence grew, and the child seemed to listen happily to the man's talk as he taxed his memory for pictures he could describe simply, using many gestures.

"Great waters and leaping waves yonder past Maldon," he said. "A ship with a mighty red sail, bellying to the wind. A shining blue hull hath she, and a golden poop full of windows astern, beneath a dangling lanthorn. And her beak dippeth deep into the sea, and the white foam rolleth away with the fairy bubbles upon the crest of it. And the wind doth sing through the ropes, and roar in the foot of the sail. Flap, crack, it soundeth, and then the black-bearded sailors run upon the deck, and pull at the ropes, and sing…. Now see, Robin, thou and I are on the ship" – he lifted the boy upon the bed – "and yonder is the sail, and there is a wounded man in the stern, one Master Foot; him we must not go near! And all about us is the deep water. Look thou over. Dost see the fish, green and shining in armour? And some have horns, and some do fly out and drop again. And yonder's an island with a mountain that burneth and smoketh at the top" – he pointed to the fire – "and yonder a great, black rock that we must not touch, lest we be wrecked" – the broken settle served for it – "and thou and I will sail on and on, till we find the harbour where the beacon is one great jewel, and the houses and temples are wrought of ivory with roofs of gold and silver whereon the sun shineth. There be groves of trees with red fruit upon them, and purple and green birds do sit therein and sing…."

The boy nestled in his arms while he imitated the birds' songs, and made the sounds of the waves and the winds. Suddenly the child pointed upwards with a look of fear. Freeman followed his gaze. A bat had descended from the loft, making a curious scraping noise as it hooked its claws into the interstices of the irregular wall. The creature hung head downwards, and seemed to regard them.

Freeman laughed. "'Tis Master Flittermouse," he said. "He walketh without feet, and flieth without feathers."

"Bad," said Robin, making a petulant gesture toward the thing with his hand.

"Why, yes, I do not love him overmuch. He is a discomfortable beast, yet God did make him. See, we will drive him forth." He picked up a clout, and rolling it into a ball, dislodged the intruder, who flew round the room once or twice, and then went out the door.

The day wore on. They had no lack of occupation, what with arranging matters in the fireplace from the bed by aid of a long ash-staff; then Freeman had to dress the child and bathe his own head; the make believe went on, the walls, the roof, the lintel, the hutch were anything but what they were.

After mid-day, when they had made their meal, Robin wandered out of doors, and Freeman watched him out of the window. The child strayed along the grassy path and gathered blackberries or picked up stones that took his fancy. The geese came about him and pulled at his coat, chuckling, but they seemed more ready to play with him that be angry with him. The white goats, tied to staples, nosed at him, and surveyed his impassively with their long, yellow eyes. Little lizards crept among the grass and cicadae cheeped ceaselessly. Freeman felt the hush and quiet of the heat of a late summer's afternoon. He began to pick out the different kinds of birds that crossed his view − linnet, blue-tit, chaffinch, goldfinch, starlings delving in the sod, a pair of noisy jays passing from tree to tree; in a distant field toward Danbury church, plover motionless; farther away, corn being cut slowly by one man wielding a sickle. He dozed for a minute, and the murmur of flies sounded like distant waters. So the hours passed....

He looked for Robin. The child was at the edge of the track that gave on the rough road leading along the Ridge, and was looking up the track, shading his eyes. Presently a bowed figure came into sight − a grey man, cloaked, though it was so hot; one that held a staff, and struck the road and the bushes every few paces. Robin was watching his approach with curiosity.

Freeman felt a certain anxiety lest the blind man should strike the child, who stood making no sound. The stranger became suddenly aware that he was not alone. He put his head sideways, listening intently. Then he was aware of a childish footstep, and a hand plucking at his cloak.

It was evident to the onlooker that some colloquy was attempted, but it seemed to fail. The stranger's hand touched the child's head, thus to realise the circumstances. Then he was led by Robin towards the cottage. The two arrived at the door, and Freeman spoke.

"Enter and welcome! I am helpless here abed, but the child is wise and hath led you hither. You will rest awhile, for the day is hot."

There was a pause, and the stranger fumbled about the door. At length the staff and a hesitating foot preceded his entrance. Looking at him, Freeman saw a slight, elderly man with long, grey hair and a thin, shaven face that had lines scored deep upon it. The eyes were blue and wide open and of a singular beauty. It was hard to believe in the man's blindness. He wore a long cloak that came to his feet, a broad-leaved hat and shoes of tanned leather with ancient buckles. He stooped much, and his white hand, thrust out from the fold of his cloak, held the wand that touched this way and that, tentatively. When he spoke, his voice indicated a quiet refinement – the voice of one used to the choice of words and to self-possession.

"Why, sir, I intrude, I fear; but the child's importunity must bear the blame. I knew not whither he was bringing me, and the blind led the blind. Ignorance and darkness, or innocence and faith – as you will. Are you sick, sir, and have you been in this case long?"

"Nay, wounded. I do not live here. I am a soldier, and crawled here for succour. There is a settle on your right hand within reach of your staff. Will not you be seated?"

The blind man removed his hat and found the seat. Robin, from a position between his legs, gazed up curiously at the eyes that were not like those of other folk.

"A soldier? I had heard of a skirmish nigh at hand. Perhaps you are from Colchester? You have news of the siege belike? I have not heard the guns."

"Nay: I would have gone thither, had it been the will of God. I was riding with a body of cavalry that was to take part in the siege, and yet... I do not know, sir, if you are for the Parliament, or the army, or the King. I think we are both non-combatants, and will not be bitter, though we disagree. It is a sorry business. My misadventures came as a result of the act of one of mine own party."

The blind man listened. His face made no disclosure of his thoughts.

"Ay, sir; in this broil friend wounds friend. Do I gather that you are for the army?"

"Faith, I am loath to disclose myself first. Shall I trust you, sir, or you me?"

The stranger waited, and seemed to listen inwardly, as to one that spoke within him.

"I am an unworthy priest of the Church of England," he said at last, with quiet dignity. "You will know that I put my liberty in your hands by the avowal. I have made it before, and have not suffered so far.... I have no cure, and indeed have had none for many years.... I am old, and may be of use on special occasions, though things of the spirit do call me, rather than· the policies of earthly kingdoms, and the vantages or persecutions of the churches and sects."

"I, too, am a royalist," said Freeman hastening to respond to the other's trust. "I was on a mission, and was let. You have then heard no tidings of Colchester?"

"Nay, no certainty, but I do think the town hath fallen. I did hear talk of the glare of a beacon northward. Truth to tell, I came hither to find out if a beacon were being builded in Danbury, or... elsewhere. Do I understand that your mission had to do with the fall of the town?"

A new interest seemed to stir in the stranger. His face did not change, but his fingers twitched. He put his hand on Robin's head, and stroked it mechanically.

"Yea; but less with the town that with Sir Charles Lucas his life," said Freeman simply.

The blind man bent forward suddenly. "You are Simon Freeman?" he asked.

"Ay. How dost know that?" The soldier was possessed of a lively astonishment.

"Myself hath a hand in the matter.... But tell me, hath the affair miscarried?" The blind man's anxiety was obvious enough now.

"I know not. I was sore wounded and crawled hither. The – householder did know of my need, and hath taken the letter to Colchester. It may be that she will succeed."

"She? A woman?"

"Ay; yon child's mother. Yet tell me how..."

"Of your courtesy, sir. Unless I err, I am at the last cottage in the parish of Little Baddow, west of the Ridge, and hard by the track. She that liveth here, as I think, is one Marabella. Is it she that hath thy letter?"

"Even so, sir. There was none other. Is it well?"

"I do think so." He mused for a moment, the blue eyes staring strangely at nothing, the finely cut features immobile, but the long fingers shifting nervously on the staff. Robin pulled restlessly at his cloak, impatient that the conversation had passed him over. Freeman waited for the man to speak.

"I have been associated in this neighbourhood with one of our bishops, who of necessity hath come and gone privily, yet who hath been occupied in his proper work howbeit forbidden – that is, ordaining men to the ministry, and strengthening the faithful that remain. This same bishop hath had advices from the Lady Margaret Cavendish, Duchess of Newcastle, having been her friend of old. I had heard through him that you, sir, would undertake the message she would have delivered to Fairfax that should save her brother's life – she doubted not but that the General Cromwell would give it on receiving of her letter – and that you would be at the oak on the Maldon road on Bartholomew Day, at noon."

"Ay, sir, such was mine order. I heard from the house at Stepney that I should meet a pedlar at the oak, and was given the countersign and a chart, though I knew the way well enough. This pedlar – he was thy messenger, then?"

"Even so. He was a priest, newly ordained, and I took part in his ordination."

"My horse failed me, and I was late by two days. Yet I did meet him, and got my letter, and joined myself to a party going to Colchester. I was shot from behind the hedge by a king's man and came here.... And Marabella hath taken the message. I cannot move yet awhile. An useless thing am I, and know not whether the affair hath sped or no!"

The wounded man moved heavily. His disquietude was evident.

The two men talked of their common interest, while the afternoon passed and the sun set. A few long clouds rose in an easterly direction and caught the red glow flung from over Chelmsford. A planet appeared, burning. Freeman noted these things casually, but the blind man caught the impression of the evening's approach by the change in the air, and the different calling of the birds.

"'Tis a strange thing that thou and I are thus met, Master Freeman," he said at length. "I think God doth mean somewhat by it. What is it, think you?"

"I know not, but I have something of the same thought, now that you put it into words." He looked round, as if suddenly afraid. "I think now that we wait for somewhat."

The old man's face became rapt. "Give me leave to be silent awhile," he said. In the silence that ensued, a curious scraping noise was heard. Freeman knew that the bat had entered and was moving in the corner. He looked that way with distaste, but could not discern the creature.

Robin had wandered toward the fireplace, and had thrust a few sticks into the ashes. Now he came back, looking at Freeman, and held his hand up, listening again. Suddenly he spoke.

"Abel," said Robin.

The silence seemed to deepen. The three remained motionless. Only the slight scraping sounded at intervals from the corner. Then, from far away came the noise of a horse's hoofs, stumbling irregularly.

Freeman strained himself to get a view of the track and inwardly cursed his impotence. The blind man rose expectantly.

"Methinks the child is right," said Freeman. "Marabella's brother hath returned alone!"

The silhouette of the horse came into his view, moving at a walk, head down, his hoofs catching the turf.

It was evident he was utterly spent. As he came nearer, the figure of Abel could be discerned crouched upon his back, his head lying upon the horse's neck, his bare legs dangling, his arms clutching the mane.

The horse ambled up to the door and stood, sweating and steaming, while the boy rolled to the ground.

He entered the cottage and remained agape at the stranger.

"What of the letter, Abel? Speak!" said Freeman sharply, his hands clutching the side of the couch.

Abel fixed his eyes upon him. "A did give un to General Fairfax his hand," he got out at length. There was a short exclamation from both his hearers.

"Thy sister, Abel?"

Abel travailed in his mind. "Her's took pris'ner. They do be goin' to shoot she," he cried, and broke out into grotesque weeping.

BOOK THE THIRD: QUEST

Chapter XIII

"WAYFARING MEN, THOUGH FOOLS"

There is little need to follow in detail the tortuous path that led to the full understanding of Abel's adventures. It would seem that, on his escape, he had plunged into the waste land adjoining the high road and, heedless as to whether he were pursued or no, had galloped madly towards the town. He had pushed his way, passing burning houses and wasted and trodden fields, through a crowd of a most varied nature – folk that had left their homes and now would return, folk that had relatives within the walls whom they were anxious about, bearing provisions of all sorts to relieve the starvation which they knew had stricken the place. In one quarter, the sky was dark with the mirk of smoke; in another, there were hoarse yells and hymns. Soldiers and civilians rested by the roadside, yet the direction in which the crowd moved was ever toward the town. He had been chased on getting near the house of the Crutched Friars, and had fled from the rough soldiers, who had taunted him because of his wild aspect and bare legs, making a circuit across the great field at the back of the abbey of Saint John, where was Lucas House, roofless and shattered by cannon.

Shaking off his pursuers, he had found the Shere Gate open, and people pressing in and out excitedly. There were pale and gaunt faces within the town, yet there was a general air of holiday among the inhabitants. Carpets of gay cloths hung from the windows along the High Street and, outside the little church of Saint Runwald, a crowd listened to a preacher calling for an acknowledgement of the mercies of God. The Puritan cavalry swept through the broad thoroughfare and overflowed the inns. The castle was the centre of interest, for the General was there, and also the leaders of the Royalists who had surrendered.

Abel, clutching his letter in his breast, had made his way to the old earthworks surrounding the castle, and had tied up his horse to an aged thorn among a large cluster of trees that concealed him. Then, hurrying to the castle, he asked people in the crowd where "General Fairfax" might be. Few heeded him, but he persisted, intent on the one idea that filled his dark mind. At length he wormed his way through the crowd till he was face to face with a row of pikemen that towered between himself and the drawbridge, which was lowered, and gave on to a Norman archway on the farther side.

"General Fairfox," implored Abel of the soldier before him.

The man turned and looked over his shoulder. A group of officers was coming across the drawbridge. In the midst was one talking earnestly, whose manner and bearing proclaimed him a leader. The soldier before Abel jerked his head that direction. "Yonder," he said.

Abel dived towards him. The guard struck at him with his pike, but the lad was quick and avoided the blow, which caught a harmless bystander full in the stomach. He cursed the soldier, and was in turn rebuked for profanity. An animated debate followed, and, during the controversy, Abel's bare feet had carried him past the guard. The boy ran like a hare toward the General.

Cries arose, and the leader was covered by one of his followers that drew sword and presented it at Abel, whose jaw dropped in lively alarm.

"Halt!" said the man. "If thou dost move a step, thou diest.... Art mad?"

Abel held out the precious letter, crumpled and stained with its journeying. "For General Fairfox," he panted. "Oh, sir, let me go!"

"Nay; put it on the point of my sword…. So. Now, whence is this letter?"

"Marabella, sir."

"Marabella? Oh, ah, hum… One of the daughters of Heth, belike. Now, what a plague, - that is, - " He took the letter and twirled it round.

"Wait," he said.

He turned round to deliver the message to the General. Abel no sooner saw his back than he made a wild spring for freedom, dived between the legs of the guard, and plunged into the crowd.

The officer to whom he had given the letter heard the commotion.

"Hold the fellow!" he bawled, thrusting this way and that. He still held the letter in his hand. Abel ran hard, not knowing whither he went. He turned eastward, and saw another crowd before him, staring at something happening at Saint James' Church. He made for the mass of people, as for safety. Then he saw what it was that took the folk's attention.

A long file of Royalist soldiers, fully armed, was marching into the church by the west door. There was a sound of clashing within the building, and they emerged from the door on the north side weaponless. The terms of surrender included this disarmament. Some of the men looked shamed, some careless, some frankly relieved; but all bore the marks of privation. Abel ran around the building and found an unused door into one of the chapels. He ran in, and cast a look round the structure. It was deplorably dismantled. Horses stood in a row in the aisle. A band of fully-armed Puritan soldiers superintended the piling of the weapons, while others lounged against the walls, or lay at their ease, mocking the defeated men.

Abel flung himself into the straw beside a horse that was lying down. He was completely hidden, and none observed him. He lay there an hour or more while the marching and clashing went on, and then stole out the way he had come. He ran round the earthworks, and found his horse. The bells were pealing in some of the spires, but they presently fell silent. Seven o'clock struck from three or four of them, and Abel mounted. A strange quiet seemed to descend upon the town, which was broken by the sharp sound of firearms from the castle. He rode his horse out to the High Street, and put him to the gallop. Again the noise of a volley of firearms sounded, and somehow it seemed to forbode trouble.

He galloped past a knot of men roasting an ox in the street, past a famished crowd being fed from carts by soldiers, past gaunt children and fierce-faced men and women with faces pinched and eyes bright with hunger. Then he issued from the town at Head Gate, past the fallen tower and ruined fabric of Saint Mary's Church by the old Roman wall.

And thus, with dizzy brain and aching limbs, the witless lad had ridden homeward, while the sun set and the stars came out, his whole purpose centred upon keeping going till he should win back; his strength sustained by the thought that he had fulfilled his trust.

Lying there by the settle, he told his tale in broken words and pictures, while the two men helped him out with questions and gentle promptings. When he came to speak of how he had heard Marabella's captors say that she was a spy, and should be shot, he wept again. Then, having eaten, and drunk mightily of goat's milk, he slept profoundly. By this time Robin had crept to his corner and lay asleep too, his hand under his head.

Freeman felt profoundly moved. He clutched his forehead and thought. This girl and this poor fool had gone on his business, to save his honour, to save a man's life. And now, was Marabella herself dead? He groaned as he thought of it.

The blind man felt for his hat, and with his staff found the open door of the cottage. He spoke quickly in the gathering darkness.

"All may be well, " he said. "I go to find out if there be tidings. Have courage."

"You will come again, sir, if it may be?" said Freeman. "I shall not sleep till I know more."

"Yea; if it be permitted, I will come again. There is a bond betwixt us that will draw us together. God be with thee, my friend."

The voice came from the pathway outside. Freeman heard him feel his way deftly, pause to catch the direction of the wind, and touch the bushes ere he came to them. Presently his footsteps died away, and the wounded man was left in the darkness with his thoughts.

The blind priest went slowly till he reached the track on the Ridge with which he was familiar. Then he turned northwards and moved with astonishing quickness. In half an hour he had reached the end of the Ridge, paused again for a moment to listen to the sound of a rising wind in the sails of the windmills near by, and took the road that descended steeply to the river. The plashing of the mill and the sound of falling water told him of his whereabouts. He hesitated and then, removing his shoes and hose, dextrously found the ford, at the side of which were large stones from one margin of the water to the other, set for the guidance of foot-passengers. He made his way slowly from one stone to the next, and finally reached the Hatfield bank. Then he increased his speed, and, with bent head, toiled up the hill in the darkness. A low rumble of thunder sounded in the distance, and a flash of lightning, invisible to him, illuminated the horizon. The wind rose and sang through the trees.

He reached the high road, and waited patiently by the steep bank. An hour passed, and only a few foot passengers went by. Then came the hollow sound of a tumbril from Chelmsford, and he listened intently. A man was urging his horse to a quicker pace. When he was nigh, the priest stood and called.

"Who be you, then? Woa, hold up, Beauty! What's to do, master? Come out o' that old ellum and let's see thee nigh mine old lanthorn. Art a pick-purse?"

"Nay, good sir; I am a blind minister of the gospel, and would fare to Colchester. I have some little money – and I do think God sent thee to help me."

"Maybe, maybe.... A minister? Good Presbyterian, belike. Why, I'm for the Parliament, and the Lord's people may enter the town that is fallen like Babylon, as I do hear tell."

"I beseech your aid, sir. 'Tis life and death."

"Oh ay; come and give thy hand. So.... Sit thou among they cheeses, master. I do hasten with them to Colchester, for I do hear great prices are to be had. There's a kid in yon hop-sack; sit not on him.... Now, for'ard, Beauty, and the Lord send us luck!... 'If the Lord had not been on our side, now may Israel say, when men rose up against us.... Hath smitten the gates of iron in sunder.'"

The carter's whip whistled, and the horse started off, the old priest disposing himself as he might among the cheeses that smelt strongly, and avoided the kid, that moved uneasily, making efforts to get out of the sack. The noise of the tumbril prevented conversation, and the old man's head bowed forward. He was either asleep or in deep thought.

Chapter XIV

IN MEMORIAM

Mistress Alice Harlackenden moved about a long, low-ceiled room in the gabled house at Lexden with some uncertainty. She had supped, and her servant could be heard in the room above, putting things together, preparatory to shifting quarters into Colchester on the morrow. She herself was engaged in a desultory way in the same occupation. On the table by the empty fireplace stood tall tapers that threw changing lights and shadows upon her womanly beauty – her fair skin browned by the weather, her wayward gold curls, her fine brows, and small mouth. Her sober brown dress with falling collar indicated the wife of a Puritan leader, but the fineness of her linen, the elegant buckles, the artless coquetry of the cap, folded over the crown of her head, suggested the survival of other and more permanent influences on her character.

She desisted from her work, and looked out of the casement window into the late summer night. The flare of fires could be seen at a distance, the rumble of ordnance being moved from a battery not far away mixed with the voices of the men who toiled at them. Footsteps passed, and scraps of talk – complaints of heat, pious gratitude for the end of the siege, occasionally a soldierly comment on military arrangements that was less pious – came to her hearing unnoticed. She was thinking of the prisoner in the cellar below, not without pity. Well she knew it was a girl in the garb of a man that was shut up there in the darkness, with every likelihood of being shot in the morning for spying. She wondered if any food had been given to the captive; she recalled the sunburn, the flush on the dark face, the brilliant

eyes, and passionate mouth whose beauty could not be hidden to the acute observer by the dust and dirt and weariness of a long ride; the slender grace and litheness of the figure that the ungainly and ill-fitting uniform could not quite conceal. She puzzled over the nature of the message that had ended thus disastrously for the messenger. She knew that, rather than be searched, the prisoner had confessed that there was no letter, and that this had confirmed the suspicion that the captive was either a runagate or some fanatic with a design on the General's life, or mission to spy out the battery.

Mistress Alice pondered what the prisoner's thoughts were, there in the dark amid the straw. She shuddered; it was no place for a girl. She herself was afraid of the dark – more especially she hated the shadow of trees at night, the gloom of a road from which the sky was excluded by spreading branches.

More than once she had regretted having tormented her husband into allowing her to be thus near the scene of the fighting. But she had always had her way with him, and she had not come hither till the danger of a *sortie* was remote. She had felt the exhilaration at times, had wisely kept out of notice, but the deepening reports of the guns had wearied her, and she felt sorrow for the besieged. She had seen, too, the wounded and dead, and had heard tales of starvation and distress that had horrified her. Then there was this. Would they shoot this poor girl near by? She could not endure the thought.

She went to the door and looked out into the passage. There was a short flight of steps at the end furthest from the street, and the cellar door was at the bottom of it, locked, as she knew, and the key in the pocket of the old soldier who sauntered up and down outside the house, matchlock on shoulder, taking surreptitious draws at a thin pipe. She lifted skirt and went down the steps. The door was strong enough, made of oak, and fast locked. She scratched at it.

Marabella lifted her aching head from the straw and listened. She had become curiously passive, her half-dreams mingling with subdued noises, the smell of the straw, and footsteps that came and went about her. She rose to her feet awkwardly in her big boots, and came close to the door, feeling her way by the wall in the pitchy darkness.

"Who knocks?" she said quietly.

"Colonel Harlackenden, his wife," came the answer through the keyhole. "I would I could help thee, but the door is fast. Have they given thee food or water?"

"The water was overset in the darkness, and I am parched with thirst. Yet is it good to know that I am near a woman. I think I am to die. Is it not so?"

"Alas! Would I might give thee hope. I will pray my husband, but he hath never let me say a word in his soldiers' matters. Is there aught to be done? The child, where is it?"

The lady without the door listened intently. The prisoner was sobbing quietly.

"Nay, I will tell thee; my name."

"Wait, ah, wait.... The sentry!" Mistress Harlackenden had heard the door of the house opening. She sped up the stair and entered her own room again, her hand at her breast. Voices and footsteps sounded without, and the door was thrown open.

"There is one would see you, mistress. What is your pleasure?"

"Who then? It is late, and I am occupied."

"A will give no name. An old man with a staff. Shall I send him off?"

"Ay; I will see none." The man withdrew, and his voice, raised in angry dismissal, was heard. There would seem to be a colloquy, and presently he returned.

"He prayeth again to have speech with you. He useth the Name of all names by which to plead. I do think he is a man of God."

The lady stood irresolute. "Why, then, let him come, and be brief," she said at length. She sat at the table, her back to the candles, in some impatience. A sound of knocking sounded without in the passage.

Presently a soft voice came.

"I beseech you, madam, open me the door. I am blind."

With a pang of self-reproach and pity, she rose, but the sentry was before her; the two men entered, the newcomer upon the soldier's arm. She nodded to the man, and he withdrew again. Then she looked at the stranger.

Hat in hand, he stood – a bowed, forlorn figure, white as death with weariness; his thin, refined features twitching, his long, grey hair falling about his travel-stained cloak, his staff reaching out tentatively for a seat, his work shoes and dusty stockings bearing witness to a long journey.

Dame Alice Harlackenden remained motionless. A strange feeling stirred within her as of some familiarity. There was a presence and atmosphere in the room she had known – ah, how long ago? She bent forward and stared at the old man's face. It seemed impossible that the bright eyes she looked into could not see. Where was it she had seen them before? … With an effort of will conquering her momentary sense of dream, she came forward and touched his arm.

"Will not you be seated, sir? There, on your left." She placed her hand upon a high-backed chair. The sound of her voice seemed to make the man catch his breath, but he moved, and, finding the chair, dropped into it.

"Are we alone, lady?" His voice swept again through her memory, like a hand upon harp-strings reviving a forgotten tune.

"Yea, sir…. Who art thou?"

He drooped his head so as to shade his face, and did not answer her question.

"I have learned by inquiry that there is a prisoner here," he said at length. "I seek to release him."

She drew herself up. After all she had been mistaken. This was no more than a royalist attempt at rescue.

"You would see my husband, sir, on the matter. He is gone to Colchester. I cannot aid you."

The man trembled a little. "The lad hath done wrong to none, lady. He came but on behalf of another, with a message to save a man's life. Mischance delivered him into the hands of those with whom he hath no quarrel. I learn that they would shoot him, even, as a spy. Thou and I, lady, must stay that wickedness!"

"Sir, you must know well that the matter lieth not with me. My kinsman, Cornet Mildmay, took him, and hath taken order concerning him. He will be here on the morrow – God knoweth I would not that the lad should die; it were pitiful – but a woman hath no say in these matters."

"It is a woman that hath been taken, lady; a woman garbed as a man. That should move thee."

"I do know it. I tell thee I would not that she should die thus. What wouldst thou? Should I betray my husband and my cause by plotting with thee?"

The old man remained silent, but his lips moved. She felt as though her defence against him became weakened. Somehow she knew that he spoke for righteousness. The feeling of having known this man in some former life came back upon her with redoubled force. She rose to her feet, and came near to him.

"Who art thou?" she asked again fearfully.

"Thou must free this woman, lady. How, I know not, but thy wit will devise the means…. I conjure thee my one whose memory hath, perchance, equal claim on thee with that of husband or kinsman."

"What mean you? Who is this?"

"Thy mother, Alice…. I am Walter Raynal."

Her hands went to her mouth to repress a shuddering cry, and she fell back from him, staring at nothing. She stood mute while the past of thirty years ago rolled back upon her…. Her mother, dear and beautiful, moving about her old home in Gracys, a tender and heavenly presence; her mother, whom she was thought to resemble – this likeness a bitterness to her stepmother, and a constant discordant thought to her father;

90

her mother, brought up from the dark pond, dead and drowned by her own act, the result of God knows what unhappiness, that brilliant May morning with its sunshine and dappled clouds.... She recalled the horror of it, as she had peeped over the oaken balusters at the trailing garments, the covered form of the hurdle borne by those heavy-footed bearers – the sobbing of the servants.... This man had known her mother!

This man – Walter Raynal. She remembered him now, her old playmate, the former priest at the chantry, her father's secretary, the poet and artist whose dextrous pencil wrought all imaginable devices for her delight – who sang songs as he bore her upon his back, who told her tales as they sat upon the stone seats in the garden, or beneath the hornbeams and elms of the great avenue – Gracys' Walk. She knew him now, and knew the familiar spirituality of his presence. She conquered the tide of emotion that rose almost unbearably, but she threw herself at his feet, and, weeping, clasped the shoulders of the frail, old figure.

"Thou, Master Raynal! O God.... And blind?"

The old man put his arms about her and set her head upon his shoulder, just as he had done thirty years before. Tears fell from his sightless eyes.

"Forgive me, Alice, that I do recall the old days. Nay, let me touch thy face. So.... It is as it was: only methinks more like thy mother, now in the Paradise of God."

"Master Raynal, wherefore did she take her own life? My father spake never of her. There were strange tales that her spirit might not rest, but wandered in the avenue.... She was good and gracious.... Tell me!"

"As an angel, little Alice. Fear not for her. She is at peace, and in the church at Baddow is a figure of her to the life. Thy father, too, and that other wife of his. I have felt it over, and 'tis wonderful.... Nay, weep not. Dost remember the faery boy in the wood that gave thee the crystal? And the man at the windmill who played with the bright buttons?... Thy half-brother, Henry Mildmay – he is hereabouts, is he not?"

"Ay. I do not love him overmuch.... And oh, Master Raynal, thou canst not make pictures any more!"

Raynal's face lighted up. "I do see more inwardly than ever I did outwardly, little Alice, though I may no longer draw pictures.... I do think that God hath used me. Some would name me 'Seer.'" And he smiled sadly.

"Thou and I must talk over the old days, Master Raynal. What is that?" A low rumble of thunder sounded, and lightning flickered behind the drawn curtains.

"Tempest," she added "Oh, selfish me, and this poor girl captive in darkness.... What's to do?"

"We must free her, 'Tis what I came for these miles, and stinted not to pain thee with old sorrows to gain mine end. Bethink thee; is she bound?"

"Nay; but locked in the cellar below. The key was in the lock, and the sentry hath it."

"What of the other keys of the house? Is it thine husband's?"

"Nay; he hath lived here during the siege, he and some others. I came but a week ago.... Wait. In the old hutch there are other keys. One may fit." She hurried to the corner of the room and, opening the oaken hutch, drew forth a large bundle of keys. She ran from the room, holding them concealed in her wide skirts. In the passage she met a serving maid, her arms full of gear.

"Wine, bread, and meat for the traveller within," she said readily. "He is blind, so tell him who thou art, and what thou hast. Deal gently with him." She saw the maid pass into the buttery, and then stole swiftly down to the cellar.

"Hist," she whispered through the door. "I do but try the keys to see haply if one may fit."

One after another she thrust into the lock. She had tried perhaps a dozen when, to her joy, the lock turned. Her strength failed a little as she pulled the door open and groped within. A white face glimmered at her in the gloom. She put her hands on the prisoner's mouth.

"Not one word," she said. "Now, listen. In five minutes I will have all out of the way. Come forth softly then. Turn to thy right at the stairhead – forget not, - thy right hand – and go to the passage end. On thy left there is a door that giveth onto the garden. Go to the farther end thereof and thou shalt find a wall.

Must strive to scale that, and then wait. One shall come to thee."

"God bless thee, lady."

"Nay, peace – and farewell." She closed the door and, leaving it unlocked, sped up the stairs again.

The old man was eating and drinking. He waited in suspense while she told him what she had done. Then he rose quietly. She knelt before him, and he blessed her.

"Find thy way to the end of the house; then pass down till thou touch the wall; bear again to the left, and pass down the wall. The girl shall be there…. And oh, remember my mother and me in thy prayers!"

She called the sentry.

"See this traveller forth," she said calmly. "It were well I did speak with him. Nay, there is wine in the flask. Come back for it."

Marabella, crouched by the wall and, shrinking from the flicker of the lightning that forewent the storm, waited for one to deliver her from the dangerous proximity of her captor's house. She heard a slow footstep, and a curious tapping that seemed familiar to her, and gave her a certain sense of fear. She listened in doubt. The footsteps were lost in the nearer thunder, and she remained immovable. The person approaching rounded the corner, hesitated, tapped at the angle, and came towards her. She rose in painful expectation.

The stick struck her foot in the darkness, and she quailed. The stranger paused

and spoke softly.

"Come, Marabella; I am here to save thee. Lead on swiftly to the high road, and strike southward."

A flash of lightning broke over all the sky, and lingered. In the momentary illumination she saw the figure clearly.

"Billy Blind," she whispered... "Billy Blind!"

Half a mile down the road, under the shadow of a twisted thorn, they waited. The heavens were overcast, and the rain swept down suddenly. They spoke nothing, but waited. Far away clocks sounded, and now and again small bodies of men tramped down the road. Once a line of guns passed, dragged by strong horses urged by the whips of soldiers. It was near midnight when the noise of a tumbril mingled with the lessening thunder, and a voice was heard singing:

"For lo, the princes of the earth
Are gathered and gone by;
Such things to see they marvelled much-
Were 'stounded utterly. "

"Come up, Beauty...

'Lift up your heads, ye gates of brass'

Woa, then...What a plague...Oh, 'tis thou. Well get ye in, and the lad too."

They tumbled into the empty cart, and lay exhausted among the sacks that had recently contained cheeses. The rain beat upon them at intervals, but they slept, while the horse jogged on through the night, and the driver sang, or talked to himself.

At dawn Marabella woke and looked at her companion. He was lying face upward, sleeping quietly. She dwelt upon the beauty of his worn features, the infinite patience of his expression – the singular peacefulness of it, as that of one dead. As she moved her stiffened limbs, he woke quietly, and heard her stirring.

94

"Where are we, Marabella?"

"Nigh Hatfield, masters," cried the driver.

"And brave news do we carry. Oreb and Zeeb – yea, Zeba and Zalmunnah – two mighty malignants, the less to fight against the Lord His people!"

"How mean you, sir?"

"Why, Colchester is taken, like Jericho, as ye know. And the men that withstood the Lord His army, Lucas and Lisle – "

"What of them?"

"Shot two days agone behind the castle, by General Fairfax his orders!"

The old priest groaned deeply, and he fell forward against Marabella's shoulder. So it had all been in vain.

Chapter XV

TRYST

A week had passed since Marabella had returned to the cottage alone. She had brought news to the wounded man of the failure of the attempt, and had said little else. His heart had leapt when he saw her, but the story she had to tell moved him to profound grief. And she seemed to have lapsed into her old defiant self, moving about the place with burning eyes and rebellious mouth.

Freeman did not enlighten her as to the character of the strange man she knew as "Billy Blind," who had mysteriously appeared to rescue her. And she, for her part, was silent about the weird experiences she had when she came upon him at the Camp. Thus there were secrets that made a barrier between them, and a profound depression resulting from the failure brooded over the man's mind, and caused him to spend long hours in fretful silence. He knew that the old priest would contrive that the true account should reach the Lady Margaret, and that he himself need take no pains on that account; but his self-esteem

had received a shock. His cold rectitude in the past had hitherto spelt success in his missions. Trust had been placed in him and in none other in the matter, and it had miscarried; the precious life was lost. He was troubled and oppressed. He watched Marabella's movements and demeanour, and she proved an increasingly disturbing element. He began to desire her perpetual presence, and looked for her impatiently when she was absent. And this impatience was a thing unfamiliar to him, since the years when the hard lessons of adolescence had schooled him to stoicism.

The child Robin proved at whiles a diversion and a bond between them. The moody reserve of both would soften under the child's artless ways and his demands upon them. Freeman could now put his foot to the floor, and his other hurts healed rapidly. He began to wonder when he should depart again to find a new mission. But, indeed, there seemed little likelihood of his being used in the service of the Royalist party in the kingdom, for its fortunes were at the lowest ebb.

In the distance, seen from the cottage, the harvesting went on, and the days shortened imperceptibly, while the cloud still hung over them. The lad Abel conceived in his slow way a certain suspicion of Freeman. He spoke little, and had a way of drawing down his thatch of hair in a sort of animal frown over his eyes when he surveyed him. In a dull way he had a conviction that Freeman was in some manner responsible for the sorrow that overhung Marabella, whom he served with a dog-like obedience; and his instinct made him aware that this mood was new, and made her different from her old self.

They discussed now and again what had happened to the letter, which, they doubted not, had been delivered by Abel, but they never discovered the truth. Whether the officer who took it had forgotten and then suppressed it; whether Fairfax himself had chosen not to admit its receipt until too late; what private explanations were required or made between Cromwell and Fairfax they never knew. And surmisings were so vain and profitless. There was the failure; that was enough.

As the days passed in the strange household, the man's cold nature underwent a slow change. He was aware of processes at work within him to which he had hitherto been a stranger. The world had been a well-organized affair in which the clash of opposing elements and ideals afforded a self-contained man, like himself, who demanded little from it except hard and difficult work, constant and absorbing activity. Foibles and weaknesses of those whose commands he obeyed, and whose interests he served, he treated with unconcerned toleration and acquiescence. They were part of the working out of a scheme for which he was not responsible. His fine, cold face expressed in its composure a certain enjoyment in its very athleticism of mind and person. But now the constant presence of the woman caused an emotional invasion that he felt as vaguely disquieting. The wonder of her femininity, the warmth and softness that pervaded the place, made a strange sweetness not unmixed with pain. She had no coquetry. Her despondency that burdened her movements, that darkened her eyes and made her lips droop, outweighed any natural instinct.

He took a particular interest in the child, pondering in wonderment over his little form and quaint gestures. The miracle of motherhood stirred within him a new sense of the marvellous that was like music. He would touch Robin when he came near, and try to realise the fact that he took his being from the woman. He had time for meditation and introspection, and his nature deepened, and yet between the man and the woman there remained a barrier, and the persistent reminder of their failure obsessed them. He determined to end the situation and to go at the earliest moment, and then he found, to his surprise, that the thought caused him a pang of sorrow. Upon one of the occasions of their guarded speech and heavy silences, the reserve broke down, and he learned more of the travail of her soul. He had been saying that he could walk, and soon would go forth to his soldier's service again, strengthening his resolve by professing it to be greater than it was in reality.

"Ay, go," she said. "There is a place for you among them that strive, or have work appointed them, or fight for their cause and die nobly…. But for me, what?"

She gloomed at him, her great eyes pools of darkness beneath the strongly marked brows, her wayward hair growing now to her shoulders, and sweeping against scarlet cheeks, her hands turned together as in supplication. She had been standing against the door looking out eastward, and the light, reflected from the sunset, illuminated her as she turned to him. He paused, leaning with his hand upon a timber joist overhead, and testing his foot by a few steps. He sensed tragedy in the woman. She seemed to disseminate a disturbing passion.

"God hath taken me up and cast me down," she went on. "I was bitter and evil – Marabella, the Strange Woman – with none to care for or to be loved by, save a babe and a witless fool.... And then, strangely, came a light of hope and a fire of courage – how, I will say not – and I did believe there was that within me that God would use, that had some kinship with what is great and noble.... 'Trouble not the woman.' ... What was't that rose in the Magdalen's heart when Christ spake that to her? ... And that very night came you to my door, needing charity and succour, and I did serve you with how great a joy, for methought God had spoken. And then the call to save a man's life, with none but I to do it! Sure I was that God would use me; glad was I of every pain and the weariness that it cost me! It was a glory to me, for God had accepted me, as I did think, and did use me in His service.... I was deceived, for I failed... and God would have none of me." She wept bitterly, and hurried out of the house.

Simon Freeman pondered in his slow man's fashion. She this was the root of the trouble with her. Now he knew he longed to comfort her, desiring to take her in his arms with a sudden uprush of emotion that bewildered him. He stumbled a few steps after her, and then sat down perforce by reason of his weakness. Presently she returned, showing no sign of her weakness, her demeanour silent and reserved as ever. He waited uneasily, hoping for a further confidence and closer approach to her, but she remained as she had been, aloof and sad. So the days went on, and he grew to love her the more, till he was well-nigh recovered.

Leaves red and golden fluttered upon the dwarfed oaks or shone burnished upon the brambles; bracken rose tall and lifeless and brown about the man as he stood upon the turf, and gazed at the grey spire of Danbury church with a great planet behind it, or eastward toward the silver waters of the estuary on an early autumn evening – the last, he had determined, that he would spend in Marabella's cottage ere he took the road for London, and resumed touch with the remnant of the secret company of his superiors, for whom his unquestioning obedience, self-control, and ready tact had been so useful. The girl was not in the house, and he felt aggrieved that she should have gone from his this last night. The beauty of the sky and the countryside were little heeded by him in the sense of regret that possessed him.

He felt a small hand thrust into his own. Robin was pulling him along the Ridge-track. The child seemed to have a set purpose in his mind. He nodded wisely, but said nothing when Freeman asked him whither they were to go.

They went on together, the man listlessly falling in with the humour of the child, who ran along beside him, talking little. They turned northward, and the purple sky above them deepened as twilight gathered. Owls called now and again, and blackbirds scolded from the bushes as they approached. A great loneliness pervaded the outlook. Above the brown common westward smoke arose, quiet and columnar; the Black Wood and the Long Wood took a violet colour, and a haze hid the distant hills.

Freeman halted once or twice. He was glad to discover that he could walk thus far without discomfort or pain. He looked at the child occasionally, preoccupied and talking at intervals.

"Whither go we, Robin? Art thou tired?"

The child pulled his hand. "Nay; yonder," he said. And so they went on together. Freeman looked up at the gathering darkness.

"Surely we should go home, Robin. Thy mother will seek thee, and think thou'rt lost." He had an odd impression that the child looked fate-led. And Robin answered petulantly, as though more important things occupied his mind, and dragged at the man's hand.

They reached the end of the Ridge where the windmills stood, a mile from home, and now the child raced on ahead in the north-easterly direction. Soon they lost the path, and Freeman, following the little figure, stopped and gazed. They had come to the Camp on Warren Hill, with its earthen walls that crowned the steep slope. Northward, the country fell away in wild wastes, and the expanse was filled with the night. He looked round curiously at the place. Robin had run to the centre of it, mounting the long barrow, and was resting himself against a young oak tree that grew from it. An unaccountable stillness seemed to fall, and the man felt a strange thrill, almost of fear.

"Robin," he called, "come back, I command thee!"

To himself, his own voice seemed to have a new note about it. The trees about the earthwork echoed his words almost scornfully. The child took no heed. He could be seen only indistinctly now, there by the oak.

Freeman pushed on almost angrily. He determined to catch the boy up and return, whether he would or no. And then a sense of unreality invaded him. He had come to the long barrow, and the earth beneath him seemed to live and move. He had the impression that he stood deep in it, or that some emanation surrounded him. He passed his hand over his eyes, thinking he had over-exerted himself, and that he was brain-sick.

The whole barrow was suffused with a silvery light, like that of moonbeams intensified. For the most part it was opaque, but in places a translucency allowed him to see the child through it, his head leaning against the tree. He was fast asleep. Freeman made a step towards him fearfully. This was magic, surely, such as he had read of. Well, he was Christian. He thought of Scripture texts that should hearten him. His fear became less, but his wonder increased.

The emanation of the light grew more opaque. It seemed to the man to be called forth by the presence of the child, for it flowed towards him, as though at the command of a magician, and eddied back in long fiery curves and folds that returned upon their source, and spread above, below, outward, and inward as though endued with multitudinous life. It seemed to burn with the radiance of a vast opal, and again the glory would subside into pure pearl. It had flecks and flames in it of blue and orange and deep red. He thought of deep seas and sunsets and of the dawn over vague distances. The appearance spread out as it were horizontally, and remained in intense and vivid movement, yet contained within a circular shape. He bent, impelled by a volition not his own, and gazed into it. Somewhat that was associated with the deeps of his own nature seemed to call to him from within it.

And now he had a sense of the flame that gathered and grew intensely. It moved with a serpentine movement and divided itself. It seemed endowed with a purposive life that had the beholder for its objective. He closed his eyes and bent to it, as it were to drink it in. A sudden shock of sweetness and strength came to him; a new life became part of him. For an instant it seemed that his old self rose in revolt, his old disciplined self that had been schooled to questionless renunciation and denial of all but the will of another. And then, like a tide of music and fragrance, a great spiritual addition came to him. He became conscious of new existences that provided unguessed experiences, thoughts, dreams, and acts that were his own, yet from which he had hitherto been debarred. The splendour became intolerable. He fell forward upon his face and consciousness went from him.

* * * * *

He awoke in the dark. A faint moon shone somewhere, and by its light he beheld the child Robin still asleep upon the barrow. The miracle was past. He gazed astounded at the dark turf that clothed the barrow, at the earthworks melting into darkness about him. He rose to his feet, and, trying to realize himself, knew he was not as he had been. His heart beat and rioted within him. His past took on new values and life new meanings. He believed himself to have gone mad suddenly, and then again was convinced that he had not known human existence till then, but had crept about, shut out from sunshine and colour and the sweet air, like an earthworm beneath the sod.

He strode forward and picked up the child, and, as he did so, the thought of Marabella flooded him. He longed for her presence, the sight of her, the touch of her, as he had longed for nothing since his birth. With the child in his arms he turned, and, aided by the pale moonlight, strode towards the Ridge-track.

There was no light in the cottage when her reached it. He stumbled within, and laid Robin down, still asleep, in his corner.

"Marabella!" he called softly – "Marabella!"

There was a movement in the chimney-corner. The soft voice of the blind priest came to him.

"She is not here," it said. "And I do think that thou hast need of me."

Chapter XVI

HADES

Simon Freeman looked at the old man curiously. He was conscious of a change in his own attitude of mind toward him. He felt now a certain resentment to one who had shared in the authority to which he had hitherto been subject. He had thought of this mysterious agent of those who secretly manipulated the operations of the cause he had blindly served, as one to whom he could only look with profound reverence and unquestioning obedience. A new life was coursing in his veins now – a doubt that challenged the old discipline as being the ideal of a man's life-story. The cold repression of emotion and passion of youth at the bidding of an austere will, for the sake of a dying cause, the denial of numberless opportunities to touch and taste and enjoy the things that called to his past youth with piercing sweetness, at the bidding of sad-faced instructors who had taught and watched and tested and moulded him until he was a perfect tool in their hands – to help create an idol that had broken miserably – was not this failure in life? He flung himself impatiently down on the settle, and longed for the presence of Marabella. There was a void without her.

Something of a change the old man seemed to notice, for he paused irresolutely. Then as unwilling to comment upon it, he began to speak.

"I am to make known to you that the company of the house of Stepney is broken and scattered," he said evenly. "The cause for which we work is for the time overshadowed. God only knoweth what the end will be. The rebels do talk of a Court to try the King. There would seem to be little use for your sword, unless you make your way to Scotland." He mused unhappily.

"Who are you, sir?" Freeman questioned.

"My name is but for your own ears, Master Freeman. I am Walter Raynal, aforetime priest of the free Chapel of Gracys. I was at Cambridge when the trouble came, and a certain Bishop employed me in divers ways on behalf of the King his cause. I have lived at Wickham, and it was there that the prelate of whom I speak gave me to know of your errand, and bade me further it. I do think it would be well if you came thither with me and awaited the turn of things. There is money."

Freeman moved impatiently. "It seemeth a poor way to win lost honour," he said. "Is not the fleet at Holland? May not I serve there? The King's majesty is at Carisbrooke. May not he be rescued? The Parliament men and the Presbyterians are angered with the Army. Is naught to be done in London? I think, sir, the leading-strings trip me."

The old man sat silently. He was evidently puzzled.

"Why, I had thought you differently minded," he said at length. "Like myself, I deemed your sole will was to act for them at the house at Stepney as they should judge. Would you be free of the work, sir?"

"I would live," said Freeman; "and thus far I have been but schoolboy and prentice to run errands and curb my will, and peer over the edge of a stony wilderness at the pleasant valley I may not know."

"You speak strangely, sir…. But, alas, 'tis a time for the breaking up of stern disciplines and high loyalties."

The old man's voice echoed in the dark room sadly. Freeman felt a touch of contrition. His mind was full of the strange experiences of the night, and he talked as he felt – a little wildly. A great desire rose in him to confide in the old priest.

The figure in the chimney-corner rose to go. There was a tapping as he felt for the objects in the room to guide himself to the door.

"Wait," said Freeman; "I have somewhat to say. I do not make confession, as I do not deem that what I have done is sin. At the least, I consented not to what I thought was evil. Yet before I speak I would have light."

After some efforts he lit a taper. The feeble illumination showed him the old man leaning forward eagerly and expectantly. The new tone in Freeman's voice had arrested him.

"This night," Freeman said, "the child led me to the old Camp at the northern end of the Ridge.... And I saw a strange fire that arose from the barrow in the midst thereof."

"Ah," sighed his hearer; "thou too – thou too!"

"And I feared greatly, knowing that the fire was not of this world. And I beheld a divided flame – and I do believe that at the dividing thereof one part did enter into me as I bent to it, drawn by more than mine own will.... Dost think me crazed?"

"Nay, well I know thou speakest truth. Myself hath seen it many times."

"Thou – seen it?"

"Yea; there only I am not blind. But go on with thy tale."

"A new life came to me – a wider life that spread to heights and depths and far-stretching horizons of knowledge and desire that my starved and confined soul had not guessed at...."

"The soul of the woman – the soul of the woman!"

"I know not what you mean, but I am not as I was. I have not lived. Yet now I know that live I must, or seek death to find life."

There was silence for a while, and Freeman found the darkness pregnant with vague mystery. Presently the priest spoke slowly, and his voice took the sound almost of a chant.

"We do live lives that are shut in from the real world, and but few gleams break through. Shadows amid a shadow world for a few brief years, we breathe to work and strive, and deem ourselves real. By this self-deception a part of eternal purpose if effected. Yet in sooth, our souls were not created with the birth of our bodies, but have a wider and deeper existence that hath been for aeons; time doth not count with them. Below the self that we know there is our wider self in a world of spirit. There, separate, yet in an intimacy of communion, our greater selves do live and burn like flames within a glory and splendour that embraceth them and giveth them life. Yet memory telleth us not of this state of existence, and we do scarce ever know of it. In that region, Christ hath chosen to make Himself known to us. When His mortal body hung upon the Cross, His soul went down into Hades and preached unto the spirits. He hath never left it, for His ascension took Him not thence. Space hath no part in His glorified nature. The right hand of God restraineth Him not."

A slow conviction began to form itself in Freeman's mind. This man is crazed! "Doth the Church teach this, sir?" he said.

"God hath led me step by step to this knowledge," said the old man. "First I awoke to the world's wonder, the beauty of form and colour, the greatness of science and the arts, the revelation of the unseen that cometh by music, the forms of truth shadowed forth by philosophy. I followed art, and from thence was led to the Object of art, and I became a priest to interpret truth to the souls of men by the readiest way that lay to hand, the Church's system. But I would believe I have been called thence, past the forms and creeds and priesthoods of earthly arrangements, to be brought more closely to the truth's self. What I tell thee of the soul is part of such knowledge."

"But the Camp, sir?" What hath that strange place to do with thy doctrine of the soul?"

"There by certain times and certain places that, by the laws of God, have a more than ordinary quality of sacrament. The old altars of the Christians had the mortal remains of martyrs and saints beneath them. The Camp yonder is such an altar, but the priesthood thereof is not in the Levitical line, but after the order of Melchisedec."

"I do not understand you, sir. May God guide us!"

"There are buried there the bodies of a man and a woman. And by some strange law, their souls may act as hierophants to certain other souls – mine, thine, Marabella's."

"She too?"

"Yea; she too hath seen the fire and the divided flame. She too hath drunk of it, and known a wider being and existence awake within her that is yet herself, even as thou hast. Yet to her hath been imparted the soul of the man – its fortitude, its discipline, its desire to serve and to sacrifice; while to thee hath been imparted the soul of the woman – its love and passion, its craving for wider experience – and what thou wilt do therewith I know not."

Simon Freeman felt the hair stirring upon his head and strange thrills passed over him. Surely this man was crazed. Was this hideous blasphemy and the inspiration of the devil? Somewhat there was, indeed, that came to him; some unguessed-at addition to his nature – yet from whence, and what was it? Was he possessed? That was the awful question. He spoke almost shrilly.

"Sir, I fear – I fear. Is this necromancy?"

"For me yon place hath been a Stronghold," said the old man. "Even as the folk of old thronged its earthen walls and found shelter therein from rapine and death, so have I gone year by year thereto while the kingdom hath shaken and the Church hath been stricken down, and guileful men of both parties have wielded power. In doubt, in temptation, in blessedness, and in sorrow, have I had recourse there, and found peace and enlightenment and a quietness of soul contemplating the passage of wild and bitter things that indeed are transitory and momentary clouds upon the sea of eternity....

"Long ages ago, as I do believe, the place was hallowed to things of the spirit. Athwart the summit of the Camp they waited for the sun to rise, and hailed its glory. It is an altar, and beneath the midst thereof were laid the bodies of the twain whereof I have spoken. It is a place of refuge, or worship, of vision. It is a Stronghold."

Some strange sense of fear and of shrinking from the unearthly rose within Freeman. "This is not lawful – not lawful, sir!" he cried. "What hath our frail mortal life to do therewith? God will punish strangely such as do pursue these things." He rose, choking. The child stirred uneasily upon his bed. From the corner of the room came the scraping sound of the bat as it descended.

The old man rose. "Deem me mad, if thou wilt," he said patiently. "Go thy ways and learn. I may not withhold from those who have been led to ask of me the secret of the Stronghold.... Farewell."

He tapped his way out into the night, and his footsteps died away.

The sweat stood upon Freeman's forehead and his heart was beating painfully. The darkness took strange shapes. The sound of the bat seemed to hint at evil. He brought himself to his feet, and strove in his mind to pray. Then, with trembling hands, he blew the embers of the fire. The flame leaped at last, and the room seemed unfamiliar. He lit another taper and felt a blessed relief from oppression. He wondered vaguely where Marabella was, and longed for her. She at least was human, weak, and of mortal flesh like himself. She would not talk of mad, unearthly affairs. Her beauty, her grace, the sound of her voice, her courage – like chords of music that rippled along his inmost nature – the impressions came and coloured his thought and wrought within him a deep desire for her.

A sound arrested him as he stood by the fireplace. She stood by the doorway, a cloak about her, her eyes burning in its shadow, and the light catching on the red, parted lips.

"Marabella, ah, Marabella!" he cried, holding out his arms to her. For an instant she moved responsive, and a deep breath lifted her breast. Her head fell back and the cloak dropped from it, disclosing the dark glory of her hair. Then the spell was broken. Robin came slowly and sleepily from his bed, moving hesitantly towards her. She caught the child to her, and buried her face in his fair hair.

A presence arose within the room, pure, austere, like a sweet and cool wind from the dawn. Freeman, was in a dream and led by an impulse he was powerless to resist, passed out of the cottage into the calm night.

Chapter XVII

TRIBUNAL

Marabella, lying sleepless by Robin's side with wide-open eyes that stared at the dark shapes faintly outlined in the little room, considered herself with a surprising detachment, and despised herself with a cold conviction.

She had not been given to introspection, nor to the estimation of moral values – a creature of impulse, of emotion, of individual outlook that admitted but one test of a person or an action, which was whether or no it harmonized with the way in life she herself had taken or perhaps been driven. Cut off from fellowship, she had built up a defence of fierce resentment toward the folk with whom she came into contact, and these were few, partly owing to her isolated dwelling, and partly to her will, no less than that of the inhabitants of the two villages, that there should be mutual avoidance.

A new power of self-judgement had sprung up within her, a sort of clairvoyance, and she surveyed her own past, her emotions, her thoughts, with a curious impartiality, and estimated them and herself by a suddenly discovered standard that found them wanting. Not only by hearsay, but by actual experience of war, she had come face to face with privation, death, mutilation, fierce ideals, and strong loyalties, beside which her own waywardness seemed idle as wind-blown spume cast in the face of one fighting for life in a troubled sea.

That strange experience within the old Camp – dream or mystic revelation, sacrament or sorcery, she could scarce tell which – she could not but acknowledge that the change within her, this invasion of an imperious law, this light that illuminated unsuspected peaks and dark recesses within her soul, had been wrought from that hour.... Conversion!... She had heard of the word, and laughed at it. It belonged to the jargon of the Ranters. But now, what was it that had come to her?

The world widened into a spacious arena wherein was being fought out a duel of agonizing significance. It was not only this miserable business of Royalist and Parliamentarians, now closing, but a deeper affair. She saw the human soul — her own, any one's — alive and awake amid a destructive environment, touched by a divine hope, inspired by a supernatural courage and endurance, empowered to rise above the fettering clog of evil and to cast aside the poisonous past that ever counselled despair. She saw the frail thing in jeopardy, in deadly peril in a hostile world, yet the fire never entirely quenched, the hope never lost, and the eternal persistence of God and His purpose in relation to it.

If this was conversion, she was converted. If it demanded humiliation, she would be humbled. Truth must be served, and the cause of the Lord upheld, whatever it might mean. Cast down utterly by her failure to save the life she had thought God meant to save by her, she had risen above the conviction that she had been rejected. She was being tried, and she would not refuse the furnace, for there was somewhat of God's gold within her wherefrom the alloy should be separated.

What to do? This man, Simon Freeman, had gone from her. That was well. She recalled his cold austerity, his single-minded pursuit of duty, his passionless though grateful attitude towards her when he had come at first. And now, there was no mistaking the authentic fire in his eyes, and in his whole manner. He loved her. She had had that disastrous effect upon this man. She had a curse of destructiveness about her. Why should a gift of God work such a thing?... She recalled her past, and Robin stirred in his sleep and she wept above him. What was this cruel power that brought strong delusion upon her and Jordan Gyll? Was the birth of Robin the aim of it all?... Her emotions surged within her, and her newly acquired spiritual power wavered like a star upon a tumultuous sea. Presently she grew quiet, and, toward dawn, slept.

She awoke with a singular determination in her mind. There was a quietness and peace about the countryside under the touch of autumn sunshine, with great while clouds moving majestically toward her from the horizon beyond Chelmsford. She noted a few folk going slowly towards Danbury church. It was the Sabbath, then. She dressed herself and the child with care, covering her unruly curls with a coif that allowed scarce anything of their dark beauty to be visible. She removed all traces of dust from them both, and the cold water had a sacramental suggestiveness about it. She tried to pray, but words would not form themselves in her mind. She took something white from the hutch, and hid it beneath her cloak. And so she went forth, holding her child by the hand.

Down the slope covered with bracken and gorse and bramble, past the Long Wood, along the red-brick wall that surrounded the old manor house of Gracys at the end of the long avenue, past the haunted pond, skirting the Black Wood she went, saying little and meeting none. She struck across a footpath that led from the old vicarage, now empty, toward the square tower of Little Baddow church, half hidden by tall elms. Passing by the hall, she came upon a small group of people in the churchyard. They were quietly clad folk – the men in black cloaks and broad-leaved hats, the women with their big linen coifs over their hair, and long white collars descending in peaks to their waists or folded about their shoulders, their skirts spreading widely and voluminously. They all stared at her in silence as she

approached, looking neither to right nor left, and entered the cool church.

It was in some disorder. The altar was moved from the empty chancel and stood in the body of the church, a plain oak table. The small altar from the side chapel was gone. The screen was broken in places, and was evidently in process of demolition. The rood she remembered, with the arms extending across the point of the chancel-arch, had disappeared. The big wall-painting of Saint Christopher still was there, but had been hacked in places. Seats were spread irregularly about, and an elderly, thin man with a long grey beard was seated upon one, reading his Bible. He had pushed his steeple-hat back from his forehead, and rested his brow upon his hand. He took no notice of her.

She heard a subdued hum of conversation break out from the little gathering near the porch. With quiet determination she glanced round, and then advanced up the church. On the north side of the chancel arch, at the angle where the wall met it, beneath the opening of the stairway that led to the rood-loft, there was a tiny seat built out that faced westward down the church. She led Robin quietly toward it, and then took from beneath her cloak what she had brought with her. It was a white sheet. Some old memory had stirred within her as to what was done when a penitent sought reconciliation to the church against whose law an offence had been committed. She placed the white sheet about her, completely covering herself from head to foot, and sat upon the little seat with Robin, whose puzzled face was pressed close to her breast, her head bowed over his. Then she waited.

There was a feeling of peace and quiet about the building, and the spoliation of much of its decoration and beautiful ornaments could not destroy the suggestion of unearthliness and awe that lingered about the carved stonework, the timbered rood, the lofty tower-arch, the colossal wall-pointing, the old tombs within the wall, the mediaeval corbels from which impassive stone faces looked down. The sunlight filtered through the windows, and long, bright squares lit the north wall; there was a rustling of leaves as the wind moved them at intervals, the chirruping of birds on the eaves, the quiet voices of the folk without. And Marabella bowed her head and waited for reconciliation.

The elderly bearded may closed his book and sighed. He had been absorbed in it, and had paid no attention to the entry of the pair. Now he stared at her, sitting there, with utmost astonishment. Finally he strode up the floor of the church among the stools and seats that were spread about irregularly and untidily, and stood before her, pulling his beard perplexedly. Marabella gave one imploring glance upward at him and then dropped her eyes. There was a noise of footsteps, and half a dozen women came in, followed by two men. They took seats, and would seem to be about to join in worship. They cast many glances at her, opened books and tried to read, while they awaited their leader; finally they gave up the attempt, and stared in cold hostility at the penitent. The two, mother and child, seemed to feel the disapproval in the air and shrank together.

"Who art thou?" said the tall elder; "and what dost thou in that vesture of Babylon?"

There was silence, broken by a woman's voice that sounded harshly.

"'Tis Marabella, the Strange Woman, Master Wilson, come hither belike to mock at the Lord His servants!"

"Nay, 'tis a penitent's robe," said a younger and milder woman. "I know her not, nor her trouble, but I do think she seeketh forgiveness."

"And hath need thereof, the wanton."

"Ah!... Dost hold with the true reformed faith, woman?"

"I seek the pardon of God and the grace of God, sir," said Marabella in a low voice.

"Why, that is well. There is surely hope for such as thou. What is thy fault?"

The unsophisticated elder with the blank expression on his face lifted horn spectacles on his forehead. Marabella flushed, stroking Robin's head. The row of people sniffed and fidgeted.

They had no need for information. Some one laughed scornfully.

"This Rahab of the hill to seek sanctification among the remnant of Israel! Is it not written that 'her feet take hold on hell'?"

"Nay, peace, wife; lest haply we be found fighting against God." The elder had a certain benevolence in his manner that did not escape his wife.

"We are come to worship and to hear the Word. Shall the Lord turn and leave a blessing? Doth not the apostle say it is impossible to renew to repentance them that have heard and rejected, seeing they crucify the Son of God afresh? Their end is that of weeds, nigh to the curse and to be burned!"

Marabella felt a weight of despondency descend upon her. Her effort towards abject surrender to the discipline of the Church of God, however difficult and with whatever humiliation, had, it seemed, been rejected. She looked up despairingly at the elder. A woman rose and began to lead her young daughter from the church with a look of indignation. Master Wilson seemed perplexed. He gazed in a deprecating way at his flock. They were moving uneasily, and it was clear to see they would not be led along the path of charity.

He frowned and bowed his head in prayer. Then, when he saw that they were all watching him, he suddenly stooped and wrote with his finger upon the ground. The allusion was not lost on them, but they did not act like their prototypes of the Gospel.

Marabella looked at the dusty pattern traced by the elder's finger. 'Go,' she read. She rose swiftly, her eyes raining tears, but with a proud and defiant look upon her flushed face. With a gesture she swept the sheet from her head and shoulders, and, taking Robin by the hand, led him away from the building.

Master Wilson rose from his stooping posture to find her gone. He had written "Go for now," meaning that she should speak with him at a future and more convenient season. She had, however, read but the first word, and taken it for dismissal. The worshippers breathed more freely when she had left the church. The sound of their voices, raised for a hymn, came to her as she passed the churchyard gate, and added to her bitterness:

> *"To all that work iniquity,*
> *Jehovah saith, 'Depart from Me!'*
> *More pure His eyes are than to scan*
> *The unredeemed heart of man.*
> *With the eternal worm they dwell*
> *That covenant with Death and Hell."*

Chapter XVIII

THE ANTINOMIAN

Simon Freeman walked with a sort of instinctive purpose possessing his feet and informing his action, of which he was scarcely conscious. The firmament spread above him, glittering, remote, enormous; the gorse exhaled a sweet and cloying perfume in the mild air, and the trees, moving gently, veiled and revealed stars through intricate patterns of branches. Stealthy rustlings of small creatures among dead leaves and bracken indicated the life of the night disturbed by his footsteps, and subdued twitterings of birds pervaded the coverts. Somewhere a fox barked and an owl called.

The whole poise of his nature seemed strangely overthrown. It was as though quiet waters that had flowed peacefully beside strong walls of self-discipline had risen suddenly with a new influx, and submerged or dissolved them. He yearned for the utmost life could give him, and felt that hitherto he had been denied much, a creature of partial realizations, or repressed impulses, or imposed, unquestioned rigours. And these inspirations and potentialities, denied their right to birth, and thrust down out of his waking life, had not died, but had waited in a sort of brooding conspiracy till chance or will should unlock the door that confined them.

Now, like a conquering army, loosed by a touch in the man's soul, new and unearthly, they had broken their bonds of inertia. His heart beat strangely. Action, danger – these had been his, but he desired knowledge and love, the communion with other existences and experiences that should contribute to a wider life, the promise of art and beauty, the enjoyment of power, the mastery of things....

He scarcely felt his infirmity as he walked toward Danbury, almost unknowingly. He descended the hill southward, and

threading his way among the waste-places, avoiding deep holes and clinging briers, seeking to quiet his tumultuous emotions by activity. Presently the ruins of an ecclesiastical building rose before him – a great arch, a fragment of a chancel. It was the deserted priory of Bicnacre to which he had come, and he wondered at the lives of those who had passed their days and nights there in quiet labour, or meditation, or idleness. He felt suddenly weary, and threw himself down, resting his head
against the crumbling masonry.

The face of Marabella grew upon the darkness when he closed his eyes and sought sleep, troubling him. Without her, existence seemed to present an intolerable want. Her strange, dark eyes and sweet mouth, her strong soul, her movements, the way she leaned this way and that, her touches upon common objects that seemed to be wonderful acts by themselves – these obsessed him. The disturbance of his nature found, as it were, a focus. He needed her, and, possessing her, all would be fulfilled. He would find completion.

He slept at length and awoke to a cold dawn, striving unsuccessfully to recall dreams of a wild, unformulated significance. He made some sort of a plan, staring moodily at the purple hills and brown slopes. He would seek service with someone of Royalist influence and sympathies, inquiring carefully where such a person might be found. Hunger assailed him, and he strode uphill to Danbury, where he thought to find food. The sun was well up in the sky, and the larks were rising and falling as they sang, when he passed the church by the edge of an old encampment. He paused to look at the immense prospect spread before him, and after a while sought the inn.

Several horses stood outside the door of the 'Griffin,' and voices, raised in dispute, came from within. A man lurched out, his face pale with wrath, his eyes flashing. He seemed a traveller on private or political business, wrapped in a cloak, with high boots covering his legs. A steeple hat was pulled down over a cropped head, and he bore a whip in his hand. He turned and shouted through the window.

"Thou blasphemous dog! Thou shalt remember thy warning in the pit!" He seized his horse's bridle and mounted with difficulty, prepossessed by anger. A noise arose from within. He spat furiously upon the ground, and, beating his horse, soon disappeared towards Maldon in a cloud of dust.

Freeman entered with some curiosity, and turned into a long, low-ceiled and wainscoted room, of which the bow-window gave on the road. A fire blazed on the great fireplace, and a crock steamed upon it. A long oaken table ran down the centre of the room, and a man who was seated at it drew Freeman's attention.

He was tall and strongly made, with wide shoulders and massive limbs that sprawled beneath the table, and upon it. His tangled hair was of reddish brown, and his dark eyes blazed with a preternatural light under heavy black brows. A short fair beard was about his lips, and his cheeks were bronzed and flushed. The collar of a leather coat was open and the great column of his neck was exposed with taut sinews as he turned his head about. He was talking rapidly and disjointedly to a group of listeners – a girl, whose open mouth and tranced eyes showed an abandonment of will and the first experiences of a visionary; a quiet, middle-aged man in brown who pulled at his lips and lifted his brows in a noncommittal way, fumbling at whiles with the leaves of a Bible; a labourer, straw-haired, red-faced, and fuddled, with the earth caked upon his legs and a bill-hook in his hands.

"Shekinah," cried the big man at the table; "if ye would know me, call me that! Baptised by the Spirit and uplifted to the third heaven, from the which I now call to ye! I tell ye, naught is forbidden to such as I. What is the Law – the Jews' Law – the Christian Law – 'touch not, taste not, handle not?' There is the spiritual fire within those whom the spirit maketh His own that knoweth naught of forbiddings and refusals and

120

the heresy of self-mortification.... What is the flesh but the temple of the Spirit? What are the lusts of the flesh but the promptings of the Spirit? 'Fulfil! fulfil!' He crieth: 'and whatsoever thou findest pleasure or exaltation in – that do.'... Life and more abundant life. The Truth maketh me free – free from disciplines and prayers and doctrines of men – papistry, prelacy, Judaism, the presbytery, the mouthers of texts and the singers of psalms!... Free? Will yet know the meaning of the word? Then owe allegiance to none, and obey naught by every prompting of the body. For what is the body? 'Tis miracle – a spiritual angel – a god, but ye knew it not, but fettered it, and mewed it up with man-made disciplines, mutilated its high efforts, and clipped its wings, thinking God was pleased therewith.... Look in mine eyes, and see why God hath wrought thy beauty!"

He bent across to the girl, who stared at him and caught her breath in a choking cry. She covered her face, lifted out of herself.

She had a swift vision of the new life that hitherto she had not known. Her inner self, veiled year by year in the past by modesty, by precepts, by pious environment, and shamefastness, clave its way through them all, ready to give and know – a butterfly bursting the chrysalis. She flung her hands across the table towards the man. Freeman, scarce knowing what he did, put his hand upon her shoulder. She looked back at him in a dazed way, her breast heaving beneath her gown, her face scarlet.

The old labourer gathered courage and came forward, tapping the point of the bill-hook on the oaken table.

"Ill talk, ill talk," he said. "Get home, Jennifer!"

Freeman nodded acquiescence to her. She searched his face, finding something there that chimed with her former woman's instincts. The man with the Bible looked dubiously at the group.

"Oh, sir," said the girl to Freeman, "if it be true..."

"True? I *am* Truth," cried the man who called himself Shekinah. "And I am Life, one with the Spirit's self – a new Adam, broke through the flaming sword-play of the seraph that scareth these slaves!" He rose to his feet and spread his arms abroad with his face uplifted.

"I see heaven opened," he went on wildly, "and the angels of God ascending and descending upon the earth to company such as are without the Law! There is naught forbidden to such as know the liberty of the Spirit…. Come!"

He turned suddenly, and the girl rose and fell at his feet.

Freeman felt a strong loathing, as for something diabolical. He drew his sword, and thrust the point within six inches of the great bulk of Shekinah, so that he could not stoop to the girl without meeting it.

He drew back snarling, and his face was like that of a beast. He crouched, ready to spring. The little man with the Bible hastened to remove himself. He made for the door, and then stayed reflectively. There was a moment's pause. Suddenly the little man caught up a large tankard of ale, he hurled it straight at Shekinah's face. For a brief instant he blenched, the blood from his forehead mingling with the ale as it poured down upon him, and then, with a roar, he leaped at his assailant. The little man bent swiftly and ran under the table. The enthusiast caught up the iron crook on the fire and whirled it round. It slipped from his hand, and with a mighty crash went through the window. The girl, affrighted, cowered upon the floor.

Freeman knew himself to be no match for this gigantic madman who believed himself to be endued with godlike powers. He therefore remained on guard with his sword, his cloak over his arm, prepared to thrust.

His opponent glared about him, wiping blood from his face. Voices cried from the road, and steps were heard hurrying into the inn. The new Adam picked up a settle and swung it about him, clearing a space, for Freeman was forced back, and the labourer with the bill-hook jammed himself into a corner to avoid the terrific weapon. Suddenly the settle follow the crock through the window, carrying sash and all with it, and through the gap went the big man into the roadway. He crashed as he fell. There was a clatter of hoofs and a string of loud oaths.

"Thou bloody-faced knave," concluded the new voice. "Stand or I have thee hanged!... God's death!"

Freeman, staring out of the ruined window, saw a red-faced cavalier tugging at his sword. The next moment he was pulled from his horse and tossed into the inn, screaming. The man endued with the Spirit hurled himself on to the horse's back, and galloped downhill. The turmoil was succeeded by an astounded pause.

The girl was weeping hysterically amid overset chairs, and the labourer gaped open-mouthed at the fallen cavalier, whose face was cut. Freeman hastened to his help, but the little man emerged on all fours from the recess beneath the table. He smoothed his hair back, and, giving his hand to a man who had hurried in, rose deliberately to his feet.

The cavalier struggled up and broke from Freeman.

"Is hell loose?" he cried hoarsely. Then he shouted to some without: "Follow that devil, and hang him if ye take him! Have a care of the mare...."

"Be you hurt, Sir Humphrey?" said the old labourer solicitously. "Surely, 'tis Satan hisself ..."

"Why, not much, I do think," said the cavalier. "But who or what is that fellow?"

The little man, who was dusting his clothes, answered him.

"'Tis an Antinomian, sir. I have heard of such as he, but did never encounter one before. He doth believe himself to be free of all Law."

Sir Humphrey Mildmay stared, and then laughed.

"By God!" he said, "the man liveth up to his creed."

Chapter XIX

THE MOUND

A small knot of staring idlers at the gate of the churchyard deterred Marabella from going out. Unwilling to pass them, she moved slowly round the church among the mounds covered by long grasses. Presently she came to the northern side of the chancel out of sight of all. A long, irregular mound lay some dozen feet or so from the wall, and she sat upon one end of it, her white sheet flung down beside her, a bitter smile upon her red lips, her dark hair shrouding her flushed face. Robin, escaping from her hand, wandered among the graves, plucking the tall cow-parsley and the cornflowers that grew here and there.

She watched him idly, and then her gaze passed beyond him to the stubble upon the fields, the trees by the river, the silver water that linked across the countryside, the rising ground opposite, Boreham Manor gables, and the stout church tower among the elms, the white clouds hurrying across the blue with the remote, motionless, feathery wisps in the higher altitudes. The fields and valleys gloomed and blazed fitfully and irregularly, as the great shadows of clouds chased across them. A heron flapped slowly across the river, giving a melancholy cry at intervals. In a corner of the field a hare shyly emerged and retreated again, and a covey of partridges whirred over the stubble and alighted, running among the straws, or huddling themselves close to the earth. A butterfly opened and shut its wings upon the wall of the church, and the peacock eyes and brilliant colours shone against the grey stones.

She endeavoured to put the humiliation from her mind. After all, who were they, these folk that she had regarded as the recipients of God's Word and administrators of His grace?

She had abased herself to no purpose. She had sought reconciliation with God, and between her and the realisation of her aim stood the Pharisees with their scorn and whisperings. She had been rejected. Why, then, she would remain outcast. She would go back to the cottage and fence herself with her pride.... And yet she knew beneath all her stormy resolves that she never could be as she had been. She had been touched with a spirit of joy in purity, and she had had a taste of the peace that passeth understanding, known only to those who set themselves to will and to do in accordance with the plan of the Eternal.... Perhaps God would show her further light, she thought. To make false steps and to err once on the road to restoration need not mean final failure.

She sat perfectly still, finding a sort of enjoyment in her own motionlessness and absorption into the life of nature about her – the story told in colour and song, the mute appeal of the dead beneath her feet. Her bitterness fell from her, and she enjoyed a strange passivity.

A sound close at hand took her attention, a persistent tapping from something that was hidden from view by the corner of the chancel. Presently the old priest she knew as "Billy Blind" appeared, his stick striking against the wall. He made straight for the long mound whereon she was seated, and sat upon the farther end of it. She had remained motionless, and he was entirely unaware of her presence.

She observed him with a quickening pulse, recalling her strange experience at the old Camp in his company. His hood was fallen back, and his long cloak shrouded him to his dusty stockings and worn shoes. His long, bony hands were clasped about his knees, and his head drooped. A skullcap covered the thin locks on the crown of his head, but over his ears and at the nape of his neck the grey hair fell about the thin face. His lips were compressed, yet moved with some hidden emotion, and now she saw that his eyes were suffused with tears that slowly welled from the lids and rolled down the furrowed cheeks.

He put out a hand, touching the turf tenderly, and seemed to stroke it, and bent as if to listen. Marabella remained as if in a trance, afraid to move, though wherefore she knew not. The old man was whispering now, and some words reached her.

"Three-and-thirty years... and still silence. Here it was they bore thee, lady.... What hath the darkness of the vault to do with thy beauty? Pitiless water, and the leading of a dream.... And though art ever young, while I that knew the benediction of thy presence and caught sight of God's beauty through thee, grow old.... Art thou quiet in spirit, lady, as thy body is quiet here beneath the grass? Hast thou been wise, and I the fool? Dost thou gaze upon God, while I wander blind among shadows?"

He bowed his head upon his hands, and little convulsive movements lifted his shoulders. Then he became quiet, as if listening, bending his face towards the earth. He seemed to hear something, for a rapt expression came upon his face. Marabella held her breath. Her thoughts suggested terrible possibilities to her. Was this strange man holding converse with the dead?

She listened, her eyes wide with fear. Almost, she thought, she too heard the distant sound of a song coming from no perceptible source. Then it died away, and the old man's face showed disappointment and woe. She made an involuntary movement, and his face turned towards her, a wild exaltation manifesting itself in his gesture. He spread his hands towards her.

"Art thou here, come back from the darkness at my poor tears? Why, that is like thee, sweet lady...."

"Ah, sir," broke out Marabella, "do not weep.... I know not of whom you speak. I was resting here by church wall on the mound, and you did come and set beside me, and I kept quiet... Forgive me...."

The old priest recoiled. "I do know thy voice. Who art thou?"

"Marabella, that saw the strange fire on the hill.... Oh, sir, what do you here, seeking the living among the dead?"

The man stood up, pondering.

"Beneath our feet," he said at last slowly, "is laid the body of the Lady Alice Mildmay. Three-and-thirty years ago they brought her from the water, and buried her here." He brooded awhile. "Myself was secretary to Sir Henry, and I did love this lady very purely and devotedly. There is no day but I pray for her, and at whiles I come here and am helped to remember.... But thou, tell me – what is this place to thee?"

"Little enough, sir, but I thought it might be.... I brought a wild and wayward heart for the ministers of God to tame. I brought a soul that sought penitence and the hard road back to the favour of God. I would ha' been ever so humble, for that I have learned to long for the company of Christ." Her voice broke, and the man turned to her with deep compassion.

"But didst thou not feel forgiveness and the new life that came to thee at the Camp – when the fire rose? – 'I will; be thou clean,' the words given me to speak were for thee, Marabella."

"Alas, sir, 'tis not enough. I would find peace with man and the Church, as with God in my soul. Yet these folk either scorn or miscall me."

Raynal mused. He felt no humiliation that his own ministry, awe-inspiring, as that of Moses on Sinai, had not fully availed to bring her peace. The thing was too terrific for her, as for the Hebrews in the wilderness. She needed a veil – the human convention and organization familiar and consented to by simple and erring. And these self-righteous representatives of it had driven her back.

"Ay, poor child," he said, 'these are too godly for thee. They will hear no confession, nor perhaps can they even perceive the pardon of God over thee that they might utter it.... Stay, it may be that I do know of some that may help thee.... Dost know of Sir Humphrey Mildmay his great house at Danbury?"

"Yea, sir. Talk was of his house being assailed, he be for the King."

"They will not hurt him, Royalist though he be, for his kinsman's sake of Wanstead, and because of his nephew, moreover, that hath a troop of the Parliamentary horse at Colchester siege.... But there be some clergy of the English Church in hiding there at Danbury. Go thither if thou wilt, and make confession, and find peace. I do think that God leadeth thee, and that He would have me help thee – at the Stronghold on the hill, and now here.... Yet leave me now alone, child. Fear not. I am no wizard or necromancer, but an old man of many memories, and this place is the shrine of them."

He slowly resumed his seat on the mound, while the girl murmured a farewell, moving quickly amid the long grass to the place where Robin was pulling flowers.

Chapter XX

STRANGE ADVENTURE OF SIMON FREEMAN

In a singular indecision of mind Freeman walked from the inn while an evening of late autumn glowed about him. The stirring encounter he had recently passed through repeated itself in his sensations, and he still trembled a little with the excitement. His reflections followed no consistent course, but swung between a practical question of what he should do, and a theoretical one of his mental attitude towards life. The two certainly were connected; for if he make his way back to his former associates, they would reasonably anticipate that his conduct and character would be consistent with what they had known before of him, and with which they had co-operated. To such, he knew that he could not now pretend. His heart was no more in the dead thing, and regret was useless.

He thought of the cavalier he had seen outside the 'Griffin' – Sir Humphrey Mildmay – and thought it useless to approach him or offer him service, even if the knight would have him. He thought of the Antinomian, and pondered over his wild ideas of the spirit's liberty. They found a surprising echo in the deeps of his own nature, and his instincts, long disciplined, woke as at a sudden vitalising. He found himself wishing that he felt the same tremendous conviction that manifested itself in the fanatic. He began to despise his own irresolution, his own divided resolves, and the indecision that resulted from his new characteristic of seeing different outlooks and vistas from a viewpoint to which he had been lifted by the invasion of a new power, and by the love he felt for Marabella.

Instinctively he turned towards the coast. There was a calm and a solemnity about the sea, lying there, wide and purple beyond the estuary, that called him. If he came to Maldon, he might discern what were best to be done. He flung his cloak over his shoulder, and strode down the road eastwards. The air thickened, and the wind fell; stars came out, and shadows deepened. At the corner of the Ridge, where the pond glimmered motionless and wan, he paused and looked northward. Not far away was the cottage in which his life had been recently spent. Marabella was there, and he was minded to go and find her. The sense that he did not know her – that there was a barrier betwixt them, set up by two opposing tendencies in their natures – troubled him. Then he thought that he would go and watch for her, to see her go by. He longed deeply for the sight of her – for his senses to report her veritable presence.... Something told him of the uselessness of that, as it told him of the futility of offering his love to her. He sighed, and went on in the dusk to Runsell Green. He paused there, for a weariness overtook him, and he felt the need to sleep. His effort at the inn and the excitement had overtaxed his resources, weakened as they were by long inactivity. He carried his hat in his hand, allowing the air to cool his forehead, to which his hair clung, wet with perspiration. A sudden determination to sleep out under the stars, a distaste for roofs and walls and company, filled him. He crossed the green and, passing a long, low farmhouse at its edge, turned down a narrow track northward toward the waste lands.

The track narrowed to a path that ended at a low gabled cottage that was uninhabited. He passed it and went onward among the bracken towards the trees. Half a mile from Runsell Green his foot struck the remains of a wall, and he found himself on the edge of a rising slope. He climbed this, and realized that the remains of a destroyed house lay about him. Irregular heaps of bricks, overgrown with nettles and rank grass, obstructed his way. He kicked against beams that crunched and yielded in a curious manner.

A strange smell was about the place, and soon he recognised it. It was that of burnt timber and thatch, and the reek of mildew, mould, and rotting vegetable matter mingled with it in a sort of deathly odour that sickened him. He could see little, but the old holly trees and dwarf oaks made strange shapes against the dark sky. He hurriedly turned from the place, and found his way carefully down the slope on the farther side.

He realised that he could go but a little farther on his journey now, for the trees inconvenienced him, the lithe twigs of the hornbeams whipping his face, and the brambles obstructing his feet. Thus he came, as it seemed, to a small clearing, at the edge of which a great oak topped a high broken bank. Beneath the shelter of this he flung armfuls of bracken and, wrapping his cloak about him, he sought sleep.

The noises of night birds came to him at intervals. Small rustlings sounded near; vague footfalls drew close and pattered lightly from him. Gossamers from nowhere fell upon his face and disturbed him. A stray insect found his hand and bit it. Frogs awoke somewhere near, and afar off a fox barked. Tired as he was, sleep seemed remote.

He opened his eyes and stared upward at the sky, vaguely lighter through the interlacing limbs of the tree above him. Things about him grew more distinct as the night wore on, for a moon had risen late. His thoughts had just enough persistence to keep his mind active, and repeated themselves monotonously. He opened and closed his eyes at intervals, and the noises of the night-life of the woods, and the pictures in his mind, succeeded one another through the interminable time. At length it seemed he slept for a while, for there was a distinct thinning of the darkness when he awoke. He looked across the clearing before him, and knew that, beyond any doubt, he was still asleep and dreaming.

About twenty yards away, framed by dark foliage, stood in moonlight a pale, slender figure, apparently that of a young child. He could see little but a vague motion, a slow grace of movement, as the figure advanced slowly from the shadows.

He listened, but could detect no sound. Then he saw more clearly.

It was indeed a child – a little girl of about eight years – entirely naked, her tiny form lithe and wavering, her dark hair falling about her face, her arms outspread, her feet making little dancing motions, her head turning this way and that with birdlike movements. She came forward with small steps, and then paused, like a thrush, listening. Then she looked up, and the moonlight caught her elfin face and revealed the laughter in it. She began to sing a wordless song.

Freeman waited patiently for himself to wake up. He shut his eyes and opened them again. The vision had not disappeared. He lifted his drawn sword and pricked his leg with the point. The sensation assured him that he was in truth awake, and he gasped at the realisation. His hair stirred upon his head, for now he guessed this creature must be unearthly. He awaited the issue in silence and motionless.

The figure stooped to a little spring and drank, flinging the water about. The man thought that never had he seen so beautiful a vision. It was, no doubt, a faery; and he wondered if it boded ill toward him. He had heard of mysterious lives of the woodland, of fauns, and dryads – this was perchance one of the latter, the spirit of some tree. He wondered what would happen if it discovered him.

He observed the thing more closely as the light grew with the coming dawn. It was apparently a child, slim to the point of attenuation, with a pale face shrouded in dark hair, through which, as the head tossed, dark eyes gleamed and a mouth laughed. He could hear now the sounds of little movements upon the bracken made by her feet as she darted about. He could not at first see what her occupation was, but at length he discovered it was the blackberry bushes to which her hands so often went, and her wordless song was interrupted at intervals as she ate the ripe fruit.

Freeman, aware that he was fully awake, marvelled. He lay perfectly still, observing the astonishing vision, perplexed that a creature clearly belonging not to the life of earth, should have need of blackberries. The thought crossed him that it was a real child, yet by what possibility might it be that such could be straying, and playing by night, stark naked and unafraid, in these wild places?

Suddenly, as the light grew, she saw him. She stood for an instant rigid; then, like a scared creature, she was gone among the shadows. He rubbed his eyes and got up stiffly. The birds were calling by now, and away to east vast crimson bars stretched across the sky. A little wind arose and moved the foliage, and an exquisite fragrance filled the world. Presently the treetops took a glint of gold that spread downward, and day had come.

The man sought the little spring where he had seen the being of his vision play. It was a rivulet, real enough, sliding over stones and moss beneath hanging bracken. He laved his face and drank of it. Then he examined the place where the figure had disappeared. He could see nothing of it, and the trees were silent of any sounds save those that were natural. Certainly the grass and bracken were bent, as though one had passed there. He stooped and looked more carefully. By the edge of the water was a small expanse of wet earth, and upon this was indented the clear impress of a child's foot.

He sat down and pondered, taking from his wallet some broken bread and meat that he had brought with him. There was a real child here, then, running wild. Was it alone? How long had it been there? How should it, thus unprotected, escape the rigour of the coming winter? The woodland and waste stretched for miles, scarce any folk ever came there, and it was well to be understood that a child, or a family, might live unguessed-at and unknown in that remote spot. He ate and drank scantily, and then, thinking to try to solve the puzzle, he followed in the direction that he thought the child had taken.

He determined that he would go through the wood and climb to a bare eminence he had discerned on the farther side, in order to obtain from thence an extended view. He scarcely knew why he should do this, but the purpose he had in mind when he set out for Maldon was shadowy and unsubstantial, and curiosity was strong in him. He had a half belief that the appearance was not natural, and the possibility of further similar experiences equally repelled and attracted.

The sun rose higher as he emerged from the trees and climbed the slope through patches of silver sand and shingle, peat that sounded hollow to the tread, having the thin roots of ling glowing from it, among bracken broken and dried, brambles with brilliantly coloured leaves and dwarf oaks. Presently he stood upon the summit of a knoll and looked about him. He soon discovered the way he must take across the waste if he would reach Maldon, for the sun caught the water of the estuary at full flood, and it glimmered on his sight away to the eastward. It was rough walking, but he resolved to go that trackless way rather than retrace his steps to the road. An aged oak, that had been riven long ago by a lightning and was apparently hollow, stood near, lifting gaunt and leafless limbs to the sky. He look at it idly, and as he did so the figure of a man strode from within it and stood regarding him.

The figure was entirely naked, brown, and sinewy; the muscle showing clearly, and the bones prominent beneath the skin. The head was covered with a thick growth of black hair that fell to the shoulders, and a long beard descended to the chest. The man was shading his eyes with both hands, for the sun shone directly into them as he gazed at Freeman.

The latter had no doubt now that he had to do either with a satyr and his family, or a madman. His mind went back vaguely to the Gospel, and the story of the healing of the Gadarene demoniac. He wondered if this creature – man or devil – would attack him. He made no movement, however, but continued to regard the astonishing spectacle.

Suddenly the figure moved toward him swiftly, and advanced within a few yards. Freeman saw with relief he was evidently human, apparently harmless, and amiably disposed. His mild, blue eyes shone through a mat of hair, and his mouth smiled. He folded his arms across his breast and began to speak. It seemed as though his English had something of a foreign accent.

"Dost seek the way of Life, brother?"

"Truly, if it may be found, friend. 'Tis a cold road if one goeth thither without clothes. Art though in it?"

"I and mine be of the new creation, brother. As Adam and Eve were in their first innocency in Eden, sinning not, so are we. Paradise is about us, the Serpent hath been cast out. The seed of the Woman hath bruised his head, even to death!"

Freeman looked round amazedly. The common did not suggest Paradise to him as he recalled the pictures his fancy created as he read the Scriptures. Then he dimly remembered hearing of a wild sect called Adamites that had sprung up in Munster and been persecuted and burnt for their mad heresy years ago. He felt some pity for this poor creature before him.

"Hast followed this way long?"

"Nay. I found the Light but three months agone; and then I followed the Lord and came out from among the lost and the fallen, the strivers for the mastery in the state, the bloody-minded, the traffickers, whom the world hath blinded."

"But thou wilt starve with the winter cold – thus shelterless and foodless."

"Oh, thou of little faith! The Father knoweth the need of His own. Did Adam and Eve starve in Eden? The sword of the seraph turneth not here. Art thou not weary of the world, and shamed of the bitter concupiscence and moiling thereof? Wherefore do the heathen hang rags of their own devising to veil the glory that God hath wrought?"

He pointed scornfully at Freeman's cloak and boots.

"Why, sir, it seemeth a convenience, and in truth I have not thought on the matter. 'Tis a habit of mine to go clothed; and I did not deem that God would be displeased with it."

"The mark of sin!" cried the man. "What saith the Scriptures? 'They were naked and unashamed'... 'Tis but the children of the Fall that go so, and go hide themselves from the eye of God and from one another! The New Creation hath risen to the perfection that God willeth!"

The man tossed his had back and spread his arms abroad; Freeman, admiring the glistening brown and ivory tones of his body, marvelled at him. Suddenly he turned and moved swiftly toward the hollow oak.

"The sacrifice!" he cried.

Freeman followed him with some hesitation, not feeling himself forbidden, yet doubting what might happen. The naked man made a gesture to arrest him, and he halted and watched. The Adamite ran to a small cairn of stones, and laid upon it wood and wild apples, blackberries, and a few foxgloves and bracken. He brought swiftly a seed of fire from the oak and lit the sacrifice. Blue smoke ascended from the flame, which soon scorched and devoured the offering. The devotee remained before it with outspread arms, his face turned upward, his long hair and beard flowing. The sinews and muscles stood out upon his back and legs.

Freeman thought he had never seen so strange a spectacle. He felt a singular distaste for it, as though he had been brought into touch with something inhuman and hateful. It was in some way monstrous, this reversion to the primitive... He turned and walked quickly away, hearing as he went the beginning of a wild chant from the fanatic.

From the top of an eminence clothed with oak he turned and looked. The man was still worshipping, the sunlight gleaming upon his brown sleekness and sinewy symmetry. He turned to continue his way. Full in his path stood the naked child he had seen before – fearless, challenging – her hands

136

raised to her eyes to shade them, her slim little figure with the changing shadows upon it. He had an impression of pearl, of old ivory, of rose-leaves, of fire in the sky-blue eyes, of shadowy tangled hair.

"Why, little one —" he said, and stopped.

A mass of bracken, nearly breast high, stood close to the child, and she had emerged from it. Now from the midst of it arose a woman's head and white shoulders. She folded her arms across her bare breast, using her long, red hair as a veil. She had pale blue eyes, like the child, and her cheeks flamed. Freeman half thought the world had gone suddenly insane, or that he was living in a particularly vivid dream. He took off his hat and stared fixedly away from the woman, who began to weep.

"Ah, sir," she sobbed; "canst help me?"

"If God will allow, lady.... Art wife to yon Adamite?"

"Yea; but this is hell and not Paradise! As thou art Christian man, think how I may get me clothes."

Freeman slowly took his cloak from his shoulders and thrust it across the bracken. She clutched swiftly at it, and he caught his breath as her beauty was revealed by the bending foliage. He turned from her, and in an instant she was covered, and stood in the protection afforded by it. From throat and ankles the cloak concealed her. Only her brown feet, hardened and weathered, showed beneath the hem, and her face, troubled, yet with an inexpressible gladness on it, looked at him frankly and gratefully. The child seemed puzzled at the transformation.

"Did not you come here willingly, lady, to this strange life?"

"Ay, sir.... I was mad. Methought, when he expounded from the Scripture and seemed to live so near to God, that he could not be wrong. We were to be leaders of a new race that should live unspotted from the world. He had a vision of Christ as the new Adam, and the Vision bade him cast away the trappings of the world — the lost world. So I believed and followed him hither, where there is loneliness, and where he said God might be found.... And I would go back to houses and streets and – other women. I am maddened with fear of the woods, burned with the sun and wind, tortured by ants....

"You would leave your husband?"

"Yea; he is happy in his craziness and nakedness. Perchance he doth find God that way, but it is not mine.... There are others yonder – two men whom he hath persuaded to come hither and be even as he." She shuddered.

Freeman felt disquieted. What, in Heaven's name, was he to do? He could not view himself reaching Maldon with a woman clothed solely in a riding-cloak, and a naked child in company. The woman wept, quietly, and looked at him for guidance.

"How think you I may help you?" he said at last.

She looked earnestly in the direction of her husband. He was out of sight, but she feared discovery.

"This way," she said, turning quickly, and following a small track downhill through the bracken and gorse. The little child ran after her, holding her cloak; and Freeman, with something like a curse, followed them. He had a sense of there being lively occurrences if any of the Adamites discovered him. He loosened his sword, thinking how detestable it would be to fight naked men, and perhaps be strangled by them.

Presently the woman stopped beside a high bank. The roots of a great oak thrust out from it, and between them she plunged, followed by the child, into a little refuge covered with foliage carefully arranged.

"None know of this," she whispered. "Follow!"

Within a bower, which was carpeted with soft turf, she set the child down, and spoke with a certain dignity that strove with shame.

"You are a cavalier, sir," she said, "and honour womanhood. Therefore it is a bitter thing to me that you should see me thus – and as yonder. I do know that God has

138

led you hither, and that you will not seek to know my name or to do me injury…. Will it please you eat?"

She set wild apples, blackberries, and an earthenware bowl of fresh water before him, and a sort of coarse bread. The child curled herself between them upon the ground, and watched him like a cat, while the mother, holding her cloak closely to her, tossed her hair back.

Freeman sat within the little bower and ate gravely. The whole thing was perplexing and beyond his experience. His thin face lit up sometimes with amusement, which he was careful to hide, sometimes was clouded with doubt as to his next move.

"I would go back, sir," the woman said at last, "before I go quite mad. If you will, you may help me…. There is a baker that dwelleth by Saint Peter's Church in Maldon, and his daughter serveth – a certain lady. If you will but seek the man, and bid his daughter tell her mistress that Eve is forsaking Eden, and doth crave that some woman's gear be brought to her at the broken cottage by Twitty Fee, why, you shall save me…. In the meanwhile, if I may but have the cloak." … She looked pleadingly at him.

He knew by the way she spoke she was no country-woman. Glad that a way had been found out for the difficulty, he rose to his feet, willing, yet unwilling to depart. The place seemed filled by her presence. A sort of music stirred his blood and ran sweetly through his veins. He flushed, and his heart beat.

She looked at him, and her eyes changed. There was fear in them. He straightened himself, and felt a new and cleaner life rising within him, and he knew that part of himself had prayed.

"I will go, lady," he said; "and you honour me by keeping the cloak. I bid you farewell."

So he bowed and went, but as he reached the entrance to the retreat he caught sight of her again. A hand was thrust tentatively from the folds of the cloak. He bent to it and kissed it. The child sat up, singing and playing with acorns.

He went out into the sunshine and covered his head.

"A strange leave-taking, by God!" he said. "And a strange world."

He strode swiftly eastwards, meeting none till he got clear of the waste-places.

Chapter XXI

THE HIDDEN MAN

Marabella made a new journey in quest of peace. It was characteristic of her – this stubbornness and fixity of purpose. There was the glimmering of a conviction that she was being led; that the crisis she had passed in the strange baptism, as it were by fire, on the hilltop, had given her a definite road to tread.

Her nature was strong, and she was convinced that by discipline and by the breaking of her self-will, she might retrace the steps of her soul's wayward straying – the fruitless wanderings along blind ways, followed heedlessly for want of a sense of any significance to life. Painfully, hampered by her want of erudition, she strove to gain enlightenment from her Bible, and at times was profoundly moved and uplifted. She prayed at whiles, using many repetitions, and this again at times helped her; but she always brought herself back to the feeling that in some way she must make atonement, and she must endure some humiliation or pain in order to come to a realizations of her soul as belonging to God, and as consciously led by Him.

She had few words for Abel, who watched her in a troubled and earnest way, his mouth open, his hair over his eyes, and his large hands picking aimlessly at the thread of his rough coat. She bade him be heedful of Robin, and went forth coifed and cloaked, her dark hair snooded, a newly washed broad linen collar falling in two long points on her breast. It was a bright autumn morning, with a few leaves, like flying gold, and great masses of rolling white clouds with spaces of deep blue sky. A wind rose and swept over the Ridge, and the elms moved as it reached them, as if in wise understanding of its message. She struck across the wastelands, passing Danbury church and the long slope of old earthwork near by, and descended the steep hill, surveying the wonderful stretch of Essex countryside before her – the violet mist rising, the blue hills lost in the distance, the tower and the chimneys of Chelmsford five miles away.

The great trees of Danbury Park shadowed her as she passed up the long approach to the house, and soon she stood looking at the moat, with the green leaves floating upon it, its broken reflection of foliage, clouds and sky. The house itself loomed over her, of massive red brick, with numerous windows and little towers. Serving men hurried about her in the courtyard; a group of bright figures stood about the bowling-green; a few ladies walked among tall sunflowers, fanning themselves. She was somewhat surprised at the untroubled aspect of the house, for the owner had supported the lost cause. She paused and wondered how she should proceed on her mission. The old man whom she knew as "Billy Blind" had told her that here were Church of England priests in hiding, and that they might listen to her, if she should open her grief to one of them; it was their duty to minister the comfort of God's Word to her. Yet how to reach these men? It was implied that they were fugitives, their orders, their services, and their Prayer Book illicit.

A noise of laughter came to her through an open window. It was evident that something in the nature of a carouse was in progress. She passed round the house and came to the chapel, a lofty brick structure having lancet windows with stone mullions. The door opened onto the pathway and she entered, sitting down to rest awhile in the empty place. The furniture was old, but tidy and cared-for. There were no ornaments, and a sort of unnatural serenity reigned. In the distance she could hear the songs and laughter growing in volume.

She determined to find a way to the kitchen, and to ask the help of any who might appear friendly. As she rose to leave the chapel, a lad came in with a besom, and began to sweep litter from the floor. He caught sight of her and paused. Then he flushed and went on with his work without taking further notice of her. She went to him timidly.

"Would you aid me, of your courtesy?" she said.

He looked doubtfully at her. "Which of the gentlemen would you speak with?" he answered.

"I am bid seek one that is a minister here. Where may he be found?"

The lad scowled. "There be no minister in this place, Madam Spy," he said. "Go your way to them that sent ye, ere Sir Humphrey come and deal with ye!"

Marabella clasped her hands. "'Fore God, I am no spy," she said earnestly. "I swear it.... Ah, do not fail me. If you but knew –" She looked at him beseechingly, and he moved about uneasily, as in doubt. Loud voices were raised a little way off and approached. The boy turned in sudden fear, and dropped his broom.

"Hadst best not be found," he whispered. "Come!"

She followed him instinctively through a door that led into the building, and entered a long passage. The sound of several men noisily making their way over the stone flags, with voices raised in careless speech or snatches of song, came more near to her. Suddenly the boy opened a door and thrust her in, closing it after her.

She found herself in a narrow and dark recess, full of shelves that bore different sorts of wines. A large butt stood in the corner, and a pipkin stood beneath the tap which dripped into it. The smell of stale liquor made her feel faint. She waited, motionless.

"As I am a sinful man," sang out a thick voice, "I saw a petticoat! Crispin, thou churlish little lecher, fye and be damned!...Crack me his pate with the jack, Roddy."

The sound of a scuffle and flying feet told Marabella of he boy's discomfiture. In great fear she sought for means of securing the door, but there was none. She cowered back by the butt, hoping not to be seen.

The door was wrenched open, and three men peered in. It was evident that they had been drinking, for their long hair was disordered and their dress awry. They pulled at one another to get a better view, leering and laughing.

"By the Lord, close to the butt of sack!... Lo you, Roddy!... Woman and wine to be reached with a single clutch!... Aw, haw- "

"All's not lost though the King's in prison. Come out, damsel, and cheer loyal hearts!"

Marabella, white and fearful, shrank from the creatures till she could go no farther.

"I would speak with the master of the house," she said at last. "Are you he?" This to the foremost and most persistent.

"I? Sir Humphrey? No, lass; but we fought together, and we drink together. He hath my fealty and I his sack." He broke into Sidney's song:

"*His heart in me keeps him and me in one;*
My heart in him his thoughts and senses guides."

The others took up the music, and they stood serenading her grotesquely, waving their arms and making abominable discords.

They finished out of breath. The tallest and most forward, a man with a little yellow beard and bloodshot blue eyes, bowed ironically.

"I do invite in Sir Humphrey's name, lady. Come forth, and maybe sing to us or dance to us…. 'Tis all the same if you seek him or me. He is abed, belike." He became coarse, and Marabella would dearly loved to have beaten him upon the mouth with her fists.

"Art Crispin's doxy?" piped the shrill voice of the third man. "A sly, discreet devil, that…. Why, he's but a child, and I a soldier of the King. Look upon me, wench!"

144

The girl looked upon him and noted his long, greasy, black locks, his thin, red nose, his bleary eyes and sagging mouth, and hated him in silence.

Suddenly the big man pounced upon her and seized her by the waist. Frantically she clutched at the butt of wine. It was not half full, and was light in consequence. It swayed, rolled a little, and fell with a crash.

The contents poured like a cataract into the room and out into the passage. The two men, starting back, fell suddenly into the flood. They swore horribly – at their own discomfort, at the loss of the wine, at Marabella's resistance. The smell of the liquor was insupportable.

The big man still clutched the girl's waist. She looked wildly for a weapon and found none. Her eyes blazed, and, could she have laid hands upon a knife, she would have stabbed him. Her breath came quickly, and tears of anger and distress rolled down her face. Suddenly she controlled herself.

"Leave go, master," she said. "I will come with ye."

He let her go, and the trio of men, two of them sodden and stinking, surrounded her as she came into the passage. They tramped along with her, leaving a wet trail on the flags, and entered a long hall, where a dozen soldiers, in various attitudes of careless abandonment, lay or sat, or slept. The long oak table was littered with drinking-vessels and flasks of wine, and puddles of liquor streamed over it, and dripped upon the floor. Two songs were being sung at the same time, and pots were hammered in time to both. Flushed faces and stupid leering mouths were turned to look as the little party entered.

Marabella was led to the great fireplace, and they surrounded her, shouting, laughing, and questioning. She stood in her quiet dress, her hands on her breast, and awaited what should happen to her.

"Hidden among the wine!" A Bacchanal in a Puritan dress, as I live!"

"Faugh, Roddy!...Get thee from me. Hast bathed in the stuff?"

"A Bacchanal! Loose thy hair, wench, or I pull the snood off thee."

A pale, poetic youth, with long fair hair and weary eyes, cried out with joy at the thought. He came towards her, and snatched at the coif over her head. It fell away, and her dark hair escaped. He threw up his hands in admiration and lurched tipsily.

"Get her the leopard-skin, Steve, from the wall. I am too drunk to reach it.... Now, lass, over the shoulder, and tie the paws, thus."

The girl remained passive under the indignity. She looked round helplessly. The men were mostly drunk and reckless. Their cause lost, they had gathered here, hoping for some sort of protection from their chief. To-morrow they might die; today they would carouse. One of them thrust a cup of wine at her.

"Drink the King his health, wench!"

She took the cup and touched it with her lips. "God bless His Majesty," she said, "and send him men of courtesy and kindness to fight for him!"

They laughed, some of them shamed, at that; and a short, square man with a red beard, who had sat with his head on his arms at the table, came forward.

"A good wench," he said. "Leave baiting her, gentlemen." He stood before her. "Now, what 'a God's name make you here?" he said, taking the cup from her shaking hands.

Marabella looked despairingly at him. "I did come, seeking a minister of religion," she said simply. "And I was told such took refuge here.... The lad found me in the chapel, and strove to conceal me in the wine room, fearing I might be mishandled.... He had reason," she added.

The soldiers looked at one another.

"How know you of the hidden man?" said the pale youth. "Go to, Dirk, let her dance for us!"

He caught her in his arms, and set her upon the table, among the wine cups, struggling. The short man called Dirk, who had seemed inclined to protect her, was thrust aside by half a dozen of his comrades. They stood around the long, disordered table closely, laughing and preventing the possibility of her escape from it.

She cowered upon the board, her hair loose, her dark beauty glowing, the leopard-skin twisted about her.

"Dance, sweetheart!... Dance for the King his soldiers," cried the big man who had discovered her; "and it may be though shalt go find thy hidden minister, if thou canst.... If not, thou must needs make shift with one of us – myself, for example." ... Somewhere a lute began to twang a blithe air. "Dance, sweetheart," came the cry again, and other voices echoed, "Dance, or be kissed!"

She stood up despairingly. Misfortune, defeat, liquor, had combined to render these men reckless and inhuman. Falteringly she gave a few steps, hoping to please them into letting her go, anywhere out of this horrible place. She looked not at the men's faces, nor listened to their clamour of applause. She listened for the lilt of the music, swaying her body and moving her feet to the rhythm. Upon the wall was a mirror, and unconsciously she fixed her eyes upon it. It reflected most of the room – the fireplace behind her, the tapestry, the weapons hanging glimmering upon the wall.... She went on moving about pathetically, with a sort of mechanical action, as though her soul was detached from her body.

Suddenly she stopped and gave a cry. From the reflected vision of the fireplace the figure of a man, clad in black, had emerged as though from nowhere. At the same time she heard a voice crying:

"Sirs, I charge you, end this lewd business! 'Tis base and unfitting. Small wonder that the Roundheads drive ye, if your spirits meet adversity thus!.... 'Not in rioting and drunkenness, not in chambering and wantonness – fulfilling the lusts of the flesh.'... Out on you! Sir Humphrey will not have it thus – to make his house a place of sin and lechery!"

The newcomer thrust himself to the table, coming from behind the girl. She bent her face upon her hands, and her heart stood still. The cavaliers laughed, and gave way rather ashamedly. They were unwilling to meet their host's anger, if he should come upon them, as this man had done. Heads were aching, and the room was in a sorry plight.

" 'Tis the parson.... Why, wench, here's thy man... Come, lads, we'll not spoil sport!" And by twos and threes they left the room noisily. The minister urged the last one with a gentle push through the doorway and turned.

"And now, thou wanton, get thee gone with thy tawdry heathenism, thy feet that take hold on hell, thy snares..."

She raised her face and looked at him, her eyes burning. Then she stood on the table, and pointed at the pale-faced man in the sober black cassock with gown and bands. She bent a little to him, her face awful and white, lifting an accusing finger.

"Jordan Gyll!"

He reeled back as he recognised her. "Marabella!" he cried. "Oh, my God – Marabella!"

They remained staring at one another, stricken by the strangeness of the encounter. A voice roared from the doorway.

"Death and hell, what hath happed here? Is my house a devil's kitchen? Who a plague art thou, thou harlot, posturing on my board?... Master parson, what is this?"

Sir Humphrey Mildmay stood there, a tall figure in red, anger upon his face as he surveyed the wreckage and confusion, and the two who still looked at one another.

Marabella spoke at length. "I will answer, sir.... I am called the Strange Woman, and I came hither, seeking the pity and the forgiveness of God, as I did think it should be ministered by a Christian priest in the house of a gentleman serving the King and the Church.... I have been most shamefully mishandled by your cavaliers – a dozen drunken villains baiting one weak woman – and for a Christian priest I find yon man." She raised her accusing hand again, and pointed at Jordan Gyll. "A betrayer of women, and the father of my child!"

She leaped from the table, flung the leopard-skin from her with a low cry, and, shrouding her head in her cloak, found her way blindly from the room and out at the great door, running wildly down the avenue under the dark trees, sobbing. Neither of the men moved to stay her.

Sir Humphrey looked searchingly at the other. Jordan Gyll was white as death, and his eyes went hither and thither. The knight laughed bitterly and angrily.

"I myself am no good man, master parson, but methinks I will seek elsewhere when I need absolution."

He strode to the doorway and called loudly for his serving-men.

"Knaves below there, clear this sty ere the ladies come."

The men came swiftly and found a strange, pale priest sitting as in a dream at the table, his head upon his hands. He did not appear to see them, but as they went on with their work, they saw him, to their astonishment, rise slowly, cross to the fireplace, and disappear within it. His footsteps could be heard dragging up the stairway concealed within the wall.

Chapter XXII

THE BAKER'S SHOP

Simon Freeman walked unchallenged into the town of
Maldon. On the road his mind was in a strange disorder. He
reviewed his adventures, and found that they had been
illuminating. He reverted to his old life of discipline, self-
control, and obedience. He thought of the little band of
thoughtful and masterful people in the house at Stepney whom
he had learned to obey, and had served with some satisfaction
in knowing that, in duty accomplished and orders obeyed and
carried out, he had not been found wanting, and had served a
righteous cause. He recalled the mission connected with the
Duchess of Newcastle and his failure in it, wondering how that
lady would receive the news of her brother's death.

Not without a thrill he remembered the scene on the
hilltop, the glance into the Abyss, the mysterious sense of
spiritual addition that had come to him, and the passionate
impulse to a greater liberty because of it. He felt again the
aspiration to a realization of his potentialities; that the
universal life of the world urged him to some self-expression
and self-realization that far transcended the restriction he had
known before. He recalled the Antinomian at the inn, and
thought that that man had travelled on the road he himself had
thought desirable. Yet it was but the liberation of bodily
instincts, he felt, with the imagined justification of religious
liberty to support it.

Liberty – the freedom to be attained by him who should so
attain truth – involved more than unbridled licence for the
body. He recalled the vision of the child in the moonlight.
There was something of magic beauty about it, a new sense of
pleasure, if it might be so called, that haunted him. What was
its nature?

Some vague correspondence rose in his mind with a song he had once heard through a window in Southwark, words and music blending perfectly, and expressing a tenderness and beauty that gave him the sense of the same magic at work. Another idea rose unbidden in his memory – a silvery picture, seen at Stepney, of some Italian girl glancing sideways, a portrait, yet with a strange power and suggestion as of being lifted above and beyond mortality....

The thought of the Adamites recurred with grotesqueness and crudity. This was what the theory of the supremacy of the body led to; a perverse disproportion that was precipitated into craziness. He would have none of that. Like Saint Christopher, he felt, he was being led to one allegiance after another. After what strange burden-bearing through storm and wild, threatening waters should the highest be revealed to him?... Meanwhile he had a mission to fulfil. He directed his way towards St. Peter's Church, and sought for a baker's shop near by.

The smell of hot bread led him to the discovery. Through a door ajar he could see an inner room, with an open oven containing lambent ashes and glowing wood. A man was thrusting a faggot into it. Brown loaves stood in rows round the low-ceiled room, and a large pasty had been newly taken from the oven.

Freeman sniffed hungrily at the inviting smell, and entered. The baker turned as he came in. He was a small man, with a pale, suspicious face, and a lock of hair that came down over his nose. Beads of sweat dropped from his forehead. His arms were bare and his shirt was unclean. He limped forward and groaned as he sat down with painful slowness, putting his hand to his back.

Suddenly a thin, penetrating voice issued from above their heads. Freeman looked about him. A narrow, wooden stairway led from the bakehouse to a loft above, and it was from thence that the sound of the voice proceeded.

"Be that Phoebe? Come, child, I do want to be rolled over!"

The baker looked despairingly upward. "Nay, mother; do ye be patient. Her'll come presently. Don't, I'll make shift to get to ye."

"I be in Christ's own comfortless trouble," said the voice. "What hinders the wench?"

"Hold yer peace, mother. 'Tis a stranger come."

"God's a stranger," wailed the unseen. "Maybe it's God.... Send the stranger to roll me over, if thou'rt too impotent. Ah-ee!" The voice ended in a shrill cry.

Freeman listened to the strange dialogue in some discomfort. He saw the baker look at him suspiciously, then at the pasty and loaves, then back to him again.

"Fear not, sir," he said reassuringly. "If you would leave the shop, do so without misgiving. I am no pickpurse or strong rogue. But I would have speech with you, when you are at liberty."

"A'll have liberty under the mowld in Peter's Churchyard and not afore, A'm thinking. Little enough speech you'll get from me there!"

"What ails you, master?"

"Ague, and a quartan, and Beelzebub athwart the loins.... Then my wife hath a palsy, and cannot move without aid, the which it do kill me to give her."

"'Twould pleasure me to serve you, if I might. I have tended sick and wounded in my time. I might lift the poor soul."

The baker looked at him, and Freeman read his thought: "Was this stranger trustworthy?"

"Who are ye, man?"

"I have been a soldier, but methinks my leaders have no further use for me. I may say I am honourable. Yet if you doubt me, I will go my way, having given my message."

"A soldier? Whose side – King or Parliament?"

"Better leave that unanswered. We might fall to strife."

152

"Nay; I am a baker, and the King's men and the General Cromwell's men all need bread for their bellies. I care not whose man you be. A'd rather bake bread than break sconces."

"Fighting is Archangels' ploy, master; while baking is Satan's."

"Art a papist? Did not the Lord bless bread? And would He ha' had it but for a baker?"

"Your pardon, master. But shall I help the poor lady to roll over?"

"Hast good thews, and dost keep thy body in subjection? Her's a woundy great woman."

"Why, master, a man can but try. Lead on."

The baker gave another searching look at Freeman. A querulous cry came from above:

"Esdras! Babble not, but come hither..... I be set fast. O Jesu!"

The baker clapped his hand to his brow, and pushed away his forelock that was wet with sweat; then he held his loins again and limped to the stairway. He began slowly to ascend by the aid of a rope, going a step at a time, with one leg foremost and lifting the other to keep it company ere he proceeded.

Freeman followed. Cobwebs drifted across his face as he made his way upward in semi-darkness. At the top of the stairs he looked round. He was in a dusky room with sloping roofs, and an uneven oak floor that gave under him dangerously. A single dormer window with small diamond panes, through which light came with difficulty on account of the dirt and the cloth patches stuffed into holes, showed a narrow bed in the corner, upon which lay a woman of large bulk. She lay on her back, her face like a pallid moon, surmounted with grey hair drawn up from the forehead and tied in a knot. Her useless hands, twisted into pathetic shapes, lay upon the coarse covering of the bed. Her eyes rolled towards him, bright and eager. The room was in utter disorder – clothes, candles, food, utensils, and broken furniture were piled together, leaving a gangway from door to bed, a path that seemed to have grown gradually narrower. The baker limped down this path carefully.

The sick woman, in pain and discomfort as she was, surveyed him closely.

"Newly shaven, Esdras.... Now, for what woman?"

"For none but thee, wife. Hush and see: here is one that will help me ease thee."

She surveyed Freeman in silence as he drew near her. Pity rose within him as he bent over her.

"I am but a poor soldier, mistress; but if I may be of service – "

Apparently she was satisfied. "Why, then," she said, "I must needs go on my right side. Do thou push my shoulder, while Esdras doth pull from yon side of the bed.... Now.... O Lord of Sabaoth!"

An enormous effort on the part of both men moved the mountainous body a little in the direction required. Then, their strength exhausted, she rolled back into the former position. Freeman felt a lively concern. He anticipated a stream of abuse, but none came. The woman closed her eyes, and Freeman wiped his brow, and then her cheeks, for two tears made a slow passage down their furrows.

A quick voice called from below: "Father, art there?"

The woman sighed with relief. "Phoebe, child – sent by the Lord's own hand.... Come, then, and swiftly!"

Light feet raced up the stairs. A girl stood among them, very small and birdlike, with bright, black eyes that searched the room and looked at the two men curiously. She was habited neatly in black with spreading skirts, and a big white collar about her neck. The exercise of running upstairs had brought colour into her cheeks, and she breathed quickly. She came forward to the bed.

154

"Which way, mother?" she demanded.

"Right side, child."

With astonishing suddenness it seemed that the girl climbed upon the mountain and perched on it. Then with a deft effort she descended again. The great bulk of the sick woman was turned with perfect ease, apparently. She sighed happily.

"Now ye may go, ye twain men-fools…. Yet I would thank you, sir."

The baker stumbled with difficulty down the stairway again, and Freeman followed him, while the girl, without noticing them, tended her mother further, tucking, patting, smoothing, and talking in a low, quiet voice the while.

"'Tis a marvel," said the baker at the foot of the stairs. "Didst see her? Like an ant with a spider's egg bag."

He subsided into a wooden settle, and pushed the door of the over to close it. Freeman felt disinclined to offer an opinion, and sat down upon a broken chair. Presently the baker, having rested, stretchedhimself carefully.

"You had some message, sir?"

"Why, yes. One that hath to do with your daughter. Is yon little maid she?"

"What of her?" The baker frowned under his forelock, and the suspicious look returned.

"My mission is to her. If it please you, I would speak with her."

The man paused irresolutely. At length he went and called up the stairway. The girl come down lightly and stood between them, puzzled. Freeman looked down at the little creature. There was a deftness and an efficiency about her that were expressed in her movements.

"I came hither to give thee a message, little one," he said. "And it is to the lady you so well serve."

Her eyebrows rose. "How do you know me, master?"

"That is of little moment. Wilt take my message?"

"Ay; if it be comely and courteous."

"'Tis all that and more, for it is to help another. The first of it is that Eve hath left Eden."

"Why, then, 'tis as old as Genesis. She did go in good company, and left better behind her."

"I jest not, maiden. The other part is that Eve would be right grateful for woman's gear, to be taken to the broken cottage by Twitty Fee."

A light spread on the girl's face; then she flushed.

"I take you, sir," she answered. "Somewhat I do know of those mad folk. They have cost my mistress many tears, and the angels of God, moreover, I doubt not.... I will take the message right willingly." She caught her cloak and sped from the shop.

The baker stumbled to the oven door, his hand to his back. "Some secret 'twixt ye?" he growled.

"Nothing dishonest, master. Wilt sell me a loaf ere I depart?"

The baker studied him. Finally he said:

"Thou'rt a broken soldier, and there will be no more fighting. Wilt stay and learn to bake and earn thy keep, and peradventure a little over if though art serviceable? Mayst learn to help me with my wife. I cannot do for her as I did use. Phoebe will show'ee the trick on it."

Freeman was silent. After all, why should he not? He had no whither to go. His money was dwindling, his old employers scattered and probably dispirited. Work of some sort would be a boon to him. The place was not too far from the Ridge. He made up his mind suddenly.

"I thank you, master; I will serve you. 'Twill be but a fool's service at first, but I will strive to better myself." He took off his coat.

The baker's face showed satisfaction.

"Why, that's well," he said. "I trust ye, for there is little harm ye can do here, even if ye be dishonest. Naught to steal. The leeches have my substance, and well are they called

156

leeches.... Now, take yon long-handled affair, and thrust it under yon loaf. Softly; 'tis not a game of bowls, that ye roll it along the floor!.... Stoop to it, for I cannot. And heed thy head among the rafters."

Freeman began to learn his new duties. It was a hot and tiring task, and by evening he was glad to stretch himself upon a makeshift bed beneath the counter. The oven glowed when darkness fell, and threw strange shadows about. Upstairs, the complaints of the sick woman sounded at intervals, mingled with the rough attempts of her husband to soothe her. He slept at length, to wake ere it was light. The baker was astir and needed him. Outside in the street the wind blew in great gusts, and rain fell heavily.

Chapter XXIII

BLINDNESS

Marabella had returned to Robin and Abel at the cottage, and had taken up her old life of isolation and endurance. The sudden flame that had lighted up within her had died down. The demand of her deeper nature for spiritual life had seemed to her to have been mocked. Her experience at Danbury Park had brought her, as it seemed, into close touch with the world's evil. Brutality and sensuality showed themselves openly and undisguised. She had been flung back upon herself. Her very effort to find the support and strength of religion had brought her face to face with her old lover as its representative.

The sight of him, the sudden recollection of their old affection – so transitory a flame, yet so dire in its results – these wounded her, and caused her pain unsupportable. Strong revulsion impelled her sudden denunciation, her tempestuous fight. To passionate disappointment had succeeded almost a spiritual lethargy. She thought dully that the call from the unseen had been a delusion, that the accession of enlightenment and will to know the strength of soul that religious teaching and discipline might afford her, had no permanent meaning or help for her. She would not deny their reality, but it was a reality, she believed, that she was not meant to enjoy.

The days grew shorter and the nights colder. One evening as she was driving the goats to shelter, she discerned Billy Blind moving in the distance, his staff feeling this way and that. He was evidently making for the Camp. She had a sudden impulse, and having secured the goats and seen Robin asleep, with Abel busy twining broom between the stakes of a hurdle, she walked swiftly to the northern edge of the Ridge. She would see again, if possible, the strange fire at the barrow. There might be a new message for her.

The lights of Maldon glimmered away eastward, and farther to the north, Wickham Bishops showed again a dull spot of fire. Overhead were brown, flying clouds, low down, and rain fell at intervals. Many of the trees were half naked, but the oaks had a thick foliage of dead leaves that rattled in the wind.

She came to the old Camp. It stood, stark and drear, in a vast desolation. Cautiously she approached. There was no light at the barrow, and with difficulty she discerned the form of the old man bent over it. She waited, but there was no movement. Once she thought she heard a wailing sound, and shuddered. She watched for an hour or more, and then, chilled, she turned homewards. So, she thought, light was denied at times, even to Billy Blind.

* * * * *

The old priest, seeking enlightenment and solace at a source from which he had hitherto derived them, found himself indeed denied. Now fields of inner consciousness had opened to him there. He had looked with the eyes of the soul into the Abyss. He had known existences, forces, personalities, experiences, far beyond all that earthly life had given him. He had deemed he had won close companionship with Christ, and that the gift of his Lord was this new opening-up of soul-consciousness. Even his bodily eyes had received new power. There, upon the hilltop, above the sepulchre of the dead, he found his departed faculty revive and act. The passing of his blindness for a space was a sort of sacrament of the spiritual gift vouchsafed to him so strangely.

But this night he remained blind. Pray as he might, no answer came. No mysterious fire arose from the barrow. No cloud lifted from his eyes. There was darkness within and

159

without, the insistent rain fell, and the chill wind blew with a wintry note. He remained there, crushed by his failure, deeply perplexed, supremely troubled. His soul had entered into its dark night.

He recalled the past – the stages of his enlightenment, his denials, his patient search, his humble acceptance of what was vouchsafed, his gratitude to God, his joy. Were all these delusions? He cried out in agonized protest against the thought. Surely it were blasphemy even to admit the shadow of doubt. Had not all his life's story tended toward the blending of the two worlds within his consciousness that he had attained?

He was conscious of a presence, there in the night, and he turned his head listening, remaining so for some time. The sense of a person imminent, of significance to him, deepened.

"Who is there?" he whispered to the night. His words were carried away by the wind, but he knew he had been heard.

"I am a stranger," answered a quiet voice that somehow thrilled him and gave him a vague sense of familiarity; "but I know thee, Walter Raynal."

"And dost thou know this place and the secret thereof?"

"Yea, and the cause of thy sorrow."

"Canst thou help me that seem forsaken, or art thou come to tempt and destroy me?"

"Is not the life of the soul won through its seeming destruction? Doth not enlightenment come as by a consuming fire?"

"Thou dost bring life and enlightenment, then. What would you with me?"

"Go back, Walter Raynal, though the past years and recall. How does thou see thyself in youth?"

"Afire with passion for beauty, and the skill of hand growing in me, so that the vision might be translated into line and colour for others to see. I did learn the language of art from my father, and spake it ever with more and more

160

confidence and sureness. Men praised me in that time, when the world teemed with artists. The beauty of men and women and children, as God made them, and the souls that dwelt within; the golden touch of light, the mystery of shadow; the placidity of the sky, the quiet trees, or the deep clouds storm-driven – the colour of woven and dyed cloths, the sheen of metal, the magic lustre and living hues of the creation – these were joy to me and became part of me as my senses rioted among them, and my deft hand set them in splendid line or glowing colour upon board or wall for the world to see!"

The old man stayed, and the wind rose and swept over the barren place. He was still upon his knees, but his face was uplifted, and his sightless eyes were fixed towards the unseen horizon, as though he looked at something beyond the blackness.

"And then, with power to achieve, came weariness of achieving. I would seek more than the world's beauty – even the Author of it. I would win behind the created to the Creator.... I sought the priesthood.... And with the priesthood came knowledge, and a joy of intimacy, as it seemed, with my Master, Christ. In the little chapel of Gracys, where I served, ministering to Sir Henry Mildmay, his sweet lady, and their dependants, I found a place in life to which I deemed God had called me. For a while I was at peace, and asked no more of life...."

"And thereafter, Walter Raynal?" said the voice of the Stranger.

"Thereafter the old passion came back upon me. My whole mind and soul saw visions in pictures, and my fingers were restless till the thought in my mind was wrought out in line and form.... The Word in me desired to be made flesh.... And the pure spiritual knowledge I had known was coloured and stained with beauty and form, music and rhythm.... I told Sir Henry I was more artist than priest. He released me from my spiritual duties, and made me his secretary. The little chapel at

Gracys was disused, and I sought God in a new way, and tried to bring others to Him...."

The man had a sudden vision, full of light and warmth, of the garden at Gracys, where the sunshine, caught by the enclosing wall on three sides, lay like a golden pool, and amidst of it the flowers glowed and burned. He saw himself, hand in hand with a little child, walking there in quiet converse with the beautiful Lady Alice Mildmay, a creature of exquisite fragility, of wistful spirituality, of piteous destiny.... The scene fled from him, and he saw her brought up drowned, from the dark pond by the Black Wood, her bright garments trailing wet, her fair hair clinging to the white forehead....

"Wherefore I left Gracys, and journeyed to Cambridge, and sought knowledge, and what others had learned of the other world; for that the dead lived, and in some manner were permitted to return, I did believe, not only by faith, but by sight also. God He knows, I sought not of idleness nor fantastic curiousness, nor that others might be in awe of me.... And some little I learned. And then it pleased God to take my sight from me, so that I read no more. Thereafter I was taken to the Archbishop, and in the troubles of the Rebellion was found useful, helping some to ordination, secretly, as was necessary; and finding shelter, first with one assembly of church folk, then with another. I could go unchallenged, being blind, where few others could, and thus I came to Wickham Bishops, and stayed....

"One night I was with a dying man, whom others would not go nigh, for that he was charged with witchcraft, and would have come before the justices had not death taken him first. He confessed he had come to know the other world in this place, within the ancient Stronghold; that the dead below were even yet a link between living souls and those that had left the body. He held that Hades was filled with the presence of Christ, who had case out Satan therefrom, and that the same Presence enfolded and gave a unifying life to the souls entering

162

there.... So the man taught and so I believed. I sought this place as the open window into Hades, and my sight was cleared – the sight of my bodily eyes and the sight of my soul.... And now blindness hath come upon me, and I am left to new terrors – of darkness, of ill winds, of bitter rains, of silence, of the sound of the voice of a Stranger whom I know not.... Art thou Death?"

Walter Raynal ceased speaking, and rose slowly to his feet. He leaned upon this staff, his head bowed down, waiting with terrible intensity, and for a while there was silence.

BOOK THE FOURTH: THE ALTAR

Chapter XXIV

THE STRANGER

Blended with the rise and fall of the wind as it roared through the neighbouring trees, or sang through bramble and bracken, seeking the drear waste of the sea, the voice of the Stranger came with a sad insistence and a haunting sense of familiarity.

"Death? Why, I do deal faithfully as he. Thou hast sought and found, Walter Raynal, but the end of the search is not what thou hast thought. The gateway to the other world hath swung open to thy touch – but *what* world?... How, with thy poor senses, wilt thou fathom the Real? For It taketh colour and presentment from the expectation of the seeker when it striketh upon human perception. Thou hast not sought in vain; but ask thyself once more – upon what realm of the spirit is it that thou has looked?...

"There is a state that lieth close to human life wherein live those Folk whom the ignorant call the Faery. They are the gods of old time, dark and light, terrible, and of utmost beauty; they know not the roadway to the Christian heaven, nor do they sink to the destruction of the banished from God. Nought that hath been worshipped or dreamed dieth. The Word of God knoweth the old dreams of man and hath given

them being, for there is nothing in the Creation of God that His Word sustaineth not. But the twain that lie here found life by their gods, and from their gods have received life. It is not for thee to know their life and their redemption. Though they woo thee to their world and it open before thee, and life and light beyond mortal knowledge flood thee, yet their way is not for thee, according to the purpose of the Eternal. Seedlike, thine immortal soul was sown into mortality, and the grossness and blindness thereof

are about it, to give it being and growth. Fear not, but when thou hast found thyself, it shall be the self spiritual."

"Have I wandered in darkness, O Stranger?"

"Thou hast found some whit of truth, but truth that it is not lawful for thee to enter into."

"Who or what hath led me to do what is unlawful?"

"The Dark Spirit. Seek no more of That. But know that the lesser redemption, whereto That would lead thee by way of Hades, is not for thee. The lesser redemption of the Faery gods is not the greater redemption of Christ."

"I would go by Christ to God, if that be His will."

"Wherein hast thou sought and found Christ that thou dost the more seek Him?"

"In the old longing for the new life, and the wild discovery, long years ago, that I was an alien in the world where sin and death are; or that sin and death are alien in the world wherein I share; in knowledge of mind and soul, that made real to me the revelation of God in the world; in painful discipline of self; in righteousness, compassion, and courage; in eager and unchecked pursuit of Truth for its own splendid sake in the world's loveliness, glowing and breaking into being about me in a myriad

of ways; in the enlightenment that hath come to me from a Companion; in the story of the life and death whereof the Gospels tell."

"Thou art not far from the kingdom. It has come to pass, that, as thou didst go, thou wast cleansed."

"Shall I turn back and glorify God, O Stranger?"

"In the way that seemeth good to thee, Walter Raynal."

"Would I might see thee. Thy voice is in a manner known to me."

"Be patient; and be at peace."

The sound as of one departing came to Walter Raynal as he stood. An inexorable sense of loss filled him. He turned and, wielding his staff, followed in the direction of the sound. Footsteps, like the echo of his own, struck on the gravel and brushed against foliage. He cried out and went in pursuit. Away from the waste hilltop, where the ancient Camp lay dark under the night, swept by wind and wild rain, out on the lonely track that led along the Ridge, he followed. At times he paused, and then again the faint noise of the footsteps led him on.

Presently a new sound, of different quality, came to him. He heard a voice call out a dozen yards ahead of him. He cried out in turn, and stumbled to his knees over a rut. A rough voice spoke:

"Hold up, man.... Art in prayer or in liquor?"

The jangling of a lifted lanthorn came to him.

"Why, God's mercy...."

"Who art thou?" said Walter Raynal as he rose, lifting his worn face, streaming with the rain, the grey hair flying about it.

"Will Treasure, o' the 'Rose and Crown,' but —"

"Well met, Will.... Tell me" — and his voice shook with a painful eagerness — "one went before me, yonder — but just ahead.... Didst see him?.... A Stranger?"

The man paused, and a new sound came into his voice.

"Ay, A saw him, as well as A see thee."

"Tell me, on thy soul, who was he?.... Didst know him?"

"Ay, A did know him, and hailed him, but he answered not."

"Who was he, man?"

Will Treasure hesitated. Then he spoke in a curious choked whisper.

"The man yonder was thou, Billy Blind!... The face I saw was *thy* face!... Why, hold up.... There, take mine arm."

166

But Walter Raynal had sunk down upon the road, his face grey as ashes under the light of the lanthorn.

Chapter XXV

A LINK BROKEN AND FORGED

Winter set in with hard frosts and snow showers in irregular squalls from the north-east. Freeman found occupation in the little dark house of the Maldon baker to fill not only the brief hours of daylight, but also the long evenings. He welcomed the bodily toil, and, though he profited little, had a quiet satisfaction in realizing that the business of his master prospered by reason of his efforts. Schooled to patience, he would often accompany the baker to the sad little upper room beneath the gables, where the sick woman lay. He was able, after a while, to help shift her when she wearied of one position. Sometimes he would read from the few books his master might borrow, and the matter of his reading was of surprisingly varied character – the Bible, a volume of Baxter, a book of Elizabethan plays.

The woman, never having learned to read, would survey him in astonishment, and forget herself in following the sentences he spoke so slowly. Sometimes he would recount his past adventures to her, amid her interjections and comments: and, upon occasion, the baker himself would appear awkwardly and tiptoe across the room to his wife's side, unwilling to interrupt. Often too, the daughter Phoebe would pay a visit, when released from her duties of attendance upon the great lady whom she served.

As to the outcome of his message, Freeman got no complete account of it. The affair had been accomplished, that he learned; but the girl had evidently been forbidden to speak of it, and he did not press her. He wondered, looking out at the snow-covered roofs and the dripping eaves, how those strange folk fared, out yonder on the wastes, and if the rigour of the winter had served to cure their heresy.

168

He pursued his varied occupations earnestly, to rid himself of his own thoughts, and to avoid realising his own desires. This was a new method of discipline, and he took to it without difficulty, often feeling a kind of ironic amusement at the way fortune had dealt with him. His whole nature at times hungered for a sight of Marabella, and then he found it almost impossible to refrain from leaving whatever work he was engaged upon, to seek her. He believed she might love him; yet, when love had hovered between

them, she had seemed to assert the utter impossibility of it. He did not know her story, and she had never enlightened him. She spoke always of herself under a dark and sinister aspect, and called herself the 'Strange Woman.' There was the child Robin, too, of whose father she never spoke. Yet he felt that there was but one woman in the world for him, and it was she.

He had pondered too, over the strange and eerie experiences he had had at the Camp. Instinctively he knew that he acquired some quality since that time that he had not known before, some will towards freedom and loosing of the fetters of self-discipline, to which he had before been a stranger. He wondered if he had been led to his encounters with the fantastic heretics at the inn and at the common as a sort of enlightenment as to what strange issues that kind of heresy might lead.

The baker would talk little of politics, but word of the King being brought to trial in London was passed round, and it was generally thought that nothing would come of it.

The year turned, and Freeman's restlessness grew from a new cause. He could not but be aware that the girl Phoebe was more interested in him than in any casual servant. Her manner of avoiding him, her quick flush when he spoke to her, the light in her brown eyes as she looked up at him, her unexplained tears, at first puzzled and then distressed him; and by her mother, lying there with perceptions in her moments of quietness sharpened by inertia, her feelings were easily read. The baker himself observing nothing, too occupied with a life filled with business, cares, and ailments of his own.

One evening, toward the end of January, the wind veered due north, and blew with a keenness of edge and a force that set the weather-wise prophesying a snowstorm. Freeman, coming in from the darkening street, met Phoebe in tears, hurrying out with her cloak about her head. He stood aside to let her pass, but got no answer to his greeting. Within doors he turned, to find that the girl had also turned on the cobbled road. She stood for an instant, as though doubtful, looking at him. Then she ran quickly
away.

He went upstairs to reach the little attic where he slept, and where his few belongings were. On the way up he passed the open door of the sick-chamber. A querulous voice called him in, and he entered. The mother was lying as usual, her enormous bulk looking grotesque in the shadowy corner, her misshapen hands pathetically inert upon the coverlet. She beckoned him with a movement of her head, and he went close to her, standing with grave courtesy, and waited for her to speak.

She was silent awhile, and then sighed.

"I can ill spare thee, Simon Freeman; but we must part."

He accepted her decision with his usual stoicism, betraying no surprise nor trouble. She looked at him keenly.

"Thou'rt no common soldier, nor rogue, so I give thee no reason, but I be not thankless.... God bless thee, and go thou on the morrow."

"Is this the master's mind also?"

"He knoweth naught, nor shall. Needs must thou feign some excuse.... Give me yon blue crock. Didst think I was so wealthy?"

She bade him empty the contents upon the bed. A large quantity of gold coins glinted and chinked upon the coverlet.

"Now, count ten o' they, and put in thy purse."

"Nay, mistress – "

"Do as I bid.... Don't, I'll – " She grew purple in the face, and her little eyes flared at him. Her poor arms jerked.

" 'Tis mine, not his, I tell thee. Say no word, but go with the daylight.... I'll not see thee again, but if prayers aid, thou'lt prosper. Now go!"

Freeman bent and picked up the coins. She nodded vigorously as he put them in his wallet; and replacing all the others in the crock, restored it to its place. Then he bent again and put his lips to the crippled fingers, forbearing to look at her face.

He found the baker stretching lean hands before a wood fire. His forelock hung as usual over his nose, and his jaws worked. Freeman looked at him with some commiseration.

"Thou must fill my place, master. I leave thee tomorrow."

The baker looked up. Expressions of dismay, incredulity, and cunning crossed his face.

"Why, not so.... Thou'rt out for a bargain, I see! Well, I will pay thee more, and thou'lt work the harder. Now, how much, think you – "

" 'Tis useless, master. I am summoned and must needs go. I owe thee much for the shelter thou didst give to a friendless man. Tomorrow I take the road."

"Oh, fool... nay, listen. I had thoughts of –"

"Say nothing, master. I go tomorrow."

"Yet bethink you of the weather; and there's the batch -"

"Give you good-night, master!"

Freeman went up to his room, but lay long ere he slept. Downstairs he could hear husband and wife in eager converse, and at times in angry dispute. The wind was rising, and shrilled round the gables. An inn-sign across the road creaked as it swung. The watchman passed, and he heard the noise of his heavy boots upon the cobbles. So the snow had not yet fallen.

Ere it was light he rose and dressed fully. He felt somehow exhilarated by the familiar sense of his sword swinging against him, and he smiled as he put his new cloak about his shoulders, recalling the fate of his old one. At his door lay a packet of food and some money. He took these and went softly down the stairway into the empty street.

He stood below Saint Peter's tower and looked down the Colchester road and up towards Danbury and the Ridge. Then he looked doubtfully eastwards, where the uniform grey of the sky was slowly lightening. He swiftly turned his back on it and strode westwards. As he did so the wind fell, and a few snowflakes drifted downwards out of the heavy sky.

Chapter XXVI

THE BEACON

The absence of any minister of religion whatever in the parish had had varying effects upon the 'Rose and Crown' Inn. It stood midway between the church and vicarage, by the roadside, and had been at times strenuously upheld by the peasantry, in whom was an ineradicable predilection for what was dispensed there, and at other times as strenuously discountenanced by a Puritan minister or local Presbyterian body that wielded discipline of varying strictness upon the villages.

Master Will Treasure, with a sort of rocklike imperturbability that was unmoved by fanaticism and rested by instinctive knowledge upon the elemental characteristics of English villagers, carried on business as he might, or closed down when he was bidden. Externally he was a silent man and made no trouble. No one knew the extent of his clandestine activities in the way of trade, but many quiet pilgrimages under cover of dusk were made by men who spoke little and smiled understandingly to one another as they foregathered in the cellar at the 'Rose and Crown,' while the front of the inn took an aspect almost of disuse and desertion.

Walter Raynal had been taken there by Master Treasure, the old man being helplessly ill, and incapable of connected thought. He lay in the front parlour, a quiet figure, going for days without speech, trying to piece together his impressions and restore his memory. In an interval of momentary lifting of the cloud, he realized where he was, and as a result a discreet messenger journeyed to Wickham Bishops and returned with a quiet-mannered may who declared himself a physician. He shook his head over the prostrate figure with the vacant eyes, and pronounced him incapable of being moved. He also gave the host money, and begged him to have a care of the patient, departing with a promise to come again shortly.

The village folk would survey Billy Blind, as they always called him, from a distance, tempering respect with awe. They had known for long his mysterious peregrinations, and some had thought him to have supernatural powers and activities; but the general opinion was that he was harmless and crazed, and was now probably quietly dying from age and exposure. Treasure's wife tended him, but he asked for nothing, and took mechanically whatever was given him – his blue sightless eyes fixed ever towards the

square of window beyond which the bare elms swayed and moved in the winter wind.

Treasure descended to the cellar one dark night, a large jack of ale in his hand, to find a small assembly of men from the village awaiting his arrival with expectation. Small leather mugs were filled and emptied in silence, and sighs succeeded. Then the host spoke.

"There's word from the Colonel, neighbours, and 'twill be in all men's mouths on Lord's Day. Maybe himself will speak in the church, after 'a's made a prayer." He gave a short laugh.

"His mother did make woundy long petitions, as I do remember," said an old man in a high voice. "A mended a spit for a lad who kept the dogs in Gracys' kitchen thirty years ago, and her did come and tell he and I about the dealings of God…. A Gurdon she was. She filled the shoes of the little creature that drowned –"

"Aw, hold thy peace, gaffer. Us have heard yon," said a short, broad-shouldered man. "What word from the Colonel Mildmay, Will?"

"The King his trial is over and done," said Treasure.

"Banished, A reckon?"

"Nay."

"Put back on perch with clipped wings?"

"Nay"

"What then?"

"To have's head smitten off," said Treasure solemnly, enjoying the sensation he caused. There was silence awhile and the others looked at him. The word had gone round that the trial was not a serious one, for that no court had the power to judge the King. They all expected a quiet and unexciting solution, after which the country would settle down, weary of blood-letting.

"Glory to God!" cried one eager voice. "the land shall have peace, and England shall be as the hill of Zion! The kings of the earth stood up against the Lord's Christ, and we have broken them in pieces like a potter's vessel!"

One or two murmured assent, but most were silent.

"Kill the King? 'Twill bring a curse, A reckon."

"Hush, man. What know us o' such matters? Colonel he says us must rejoice therefore."

"Rejoice? With the drink forbidden? A poor tale."

"Nay; build a beacon and set fire thereto, when the word come."

"Like Elijah on Carmel. I doubt me the Lord will give a sign to us. Do, I'll turn Brownist!"

"Us must do it to-morrow, or be called malcontents, and have the place searched, belike. They elders might find summat."

"God forbid!.... Build a beacon-fire, say you?"

"An' no mistake."

"Where, then?"

"Baddow Hill, I rackon, by th' old Camp. Then, when the word cometh and we see Danbury and Burntwood alight, we fire 'un."

"Ay, well; 'twill keep us warm this plaguy weather. Hither we come at noon to-morrow, neighbours; is't agreed on? And, gaffer, do ye rest here and tend Billy Blind. Thine old legs will not carry thee up the hill."

"I'll not come, if Cromwell himself told me! Many a time have I prayed for King Charlie in church, and I'll light no fire to rejoice at his killing.... 'Tis a bloody generation."

"Peace, yet old malignant. The Fifth Monarchy shall be set up. Think on the horns of the beast in Daniel!"

"Devil spit thee on each in turn, thou sour hypocrite. A would heave my pot at thee, if it were empty, which, thank God, it ain't!"

"Leave the old carle, Enoch.... Hearken what's afoot?"

A subdued murmur came from overhead.

"Billy Blind's talking to hisself. 'S' a wizard, I reckon."

Treasure moved to the stairway.

"Softly, neighbours; there's one with he."

He went quietly to the door of the room where the old man was lying, and bent to the keyhole. A high whisper filled the place.

"... Confess to God Almighty, Father, Son, and Holy Ghost, and to thee, my father, that I have sinned, through my fault, through my fault, through my exceeding fault... *Mea culpa, mea maxima culpa.*" The words were lost in a fit of coughing that seemed as it if would be the end of the old man. But presently he went on:

"*Nefas est.*... If the blind lead the blind... I have made the blind to go out of his way... They must be warned. Tell them, father" – the voice rose startlingly – "tell them, father, to go no more to the hilltop! Never, never, never!... Thou must warn them. I cannot die in peace else."

"Warn whom, sir?" Treasure started on hearing a strange voice in the room. Silence succeeded.

"His name is gone from me. Thou knowest.... The letter... The man at the oak from the house in Stepney."

"Ah, I know him. But where, in Heaven's name do I find him?"

176

"Find him – find him!... Never more to seek the flame.....
And the woman too –" The voice died away into meaningless
mutterings.

"A woman? What woman?"

"The woman on the Ridge – the Strange Woman – Mara –
Marabella."

"Marabella!... Oh, my God!"

The stranger had risen to his feet. "What of Marabella,
sir?" he whispered at last in a tense voice. No answer came.
Treasure left the door and went round by the front of the
house. He would see this stranger.

The door opened quietly and he came out, a slight figure,
pulling his hat down and adjusting his cloak about his
shoulders. Treasure stopped his way. The snow began falling
lightly.

"I should know your voice, master. Be you from
hereabouts?"

"Nay; I came to visit the old man. The leech sent me. I
have money for his keep; there, take it."

"Methinks he will want no more, save to pay for the
burying. 'Twere pity if he died not in peace."

"What is that to thee? Spying, belike?"

"I take thee for a priest. Nay, fear not – thought the
Colonel would have somewhat to say to thee. And what hast
thou to do with –"

But Jordan Gyll thrust past the man and hurried up the
road.

Chapter XXVII

REFUGE

Near the summit of the Ridge at its northern end, and on the western slope, a hundred yards of so from the track, stood a venerable oak tree. It marked the edge of the wood composed of lesser trees, and its huge growth projected like a bastion into waste lands that formed a battlefield, whereon the ancient strife of briers and broom, bracken and gorse, was fought.

Only a fragment of the oak was still alive, a solitary bough drawing life mysteriously from channels still unstopped. Year by year the living portion thrust out its yellow leaves, struggling through enormous boughs that folded upon themselves strangely, and grew a feeble crop of acorns, fighting a losing battle, and yielding little by little, as its neighbours had done through the long years. The bulk of the tree was dead, but, in the manner of oaks, the branches that had spread so long ago and died had not fallen to

decay, but had shrunken and twisted, making grotesque shapes like limbs of wrought-iron, whereon the sinews and muscles stood out, with the broken ends like giant fingers thrust up menacingly to the sky. One side had been stricken by the levin, and a dull black stain showed there. On the northern side the rains and damp had encouraged a growth of lichen and moss, unwithered by the southern sun, of a beautiful green hue. A single horizontal branch thrust out, as if to fend off a strong holly. And on one of the upper branches a carrion crow sat and called persistently.

The snow lay already some inches deep on the ground, and the grey sky seemed to bend lower with the weight of its burden. White ridges lay upon the upper edges of the boughs and branches, and on the side of the trunk exposed to the storm. The snowflakes, driven by the wind, fell thickly, and, with every violent squall, were carried along almost horizontally. The branch upon which the crow sat swayed at times so strongly that the bird was dislodged and flapped about to retain its balance. It returned,

however, to its perch, and croaked its hoarse note at intervals.

It was at the close of a short winter's afternoon, and the Ridge was devoid of humanity, save for one woman. Marabella had come forth to find some respite from her tumultuous thoughts in physical battle with the elements. The wind struck her at times like a blow, and the snow almost seemed to cut her face, so whipped and stung was she by its keenness. She kept her cloak about her with difficulty, her hair blowing about in wisps. She bent as she advanced, and thrust herself with a sort of joy against what seemed an opponent.

The windmills, like motionless giants, bore burdens of snow, and their sails were set so that they might not turn. They creaked and whistled in the gusts of wind, the hornbeams sang shrilly in the wood, and the dried, unfallen oak-leaves rustled. Beneath her feet the snow crunched and gave, and, as it fell more thickly, made walking more difficult. She needed rest, and looked round for refuge.

The sound of the crow's calling took her attention, and she noticed the bulk of the dead oak. The side of it away from the wind would afford temporary shelter. She reached it, and finding herself in comparative quietness, and able to breathe more freely, loosed her cloak as she leaned against the great bole. The crow perceived her approach, and flapped away to the wood. She could hear its continued croaking, however, some little distance away.

In a great loneliness, upon an eyrie, as it were, above the quiet plains where the houses nestled under their thatches, with the distances obscured now by thick haze and snow-clouds, yet, as she knew, spreading on three sides for many miles, she strove to feel the presence of God, and to grasp the clue to her own destiny, and the strange and wayward journeyings of her soul. She stared at the white desolation, her black eyes no longer defiant and challenging, but wistful, almost despairing.

Next she bethought her of Robin at home with the half-witted Abel, and approached a determination to suppress all aspirations, efforts, and spiritual seekings in the single pursuit of his well-being. It was enough for her, should he grow to be a man, brave and strong, who might take a man's place in the world. She would recall the past but once, in a sort of penitential review, ere she killed it.

She stood very still under the oak while the storm swept above and about her. Presently the snow ceased and the cold intensified. From the white surface at her feet, little wisps blew and made tiny drifts against any obstacle that impeded them. Dead bracken leaves were relieved of their temporary burden and stood upright again; other more substantial growths caught a new weight and bowed beneath it.

Darkness began to gather quickly, and she thought of turning homeward. She pulled her hood together at her throat, and pushed the wet wisps of hair back from her face, stung to bright colour by the weather. A creaking sound caught her attention on the farther side of the tree, and suddenly a man stood before her.

* * * * *

Freeman strode through the light snowfall that steadily increased as he proceeded westwards. He reflected on the irony of things, in that he was going from a woman who loved him too well, and whose love he neither sought nor desired, to a woman whose love he longed for, yet who, to all appearances, could meet his longing with no sort of answering emotion. Despite reason and the prompting of the more practical side of his character, his instinct impelled him to see Marabella once more ere he parted from her for ever, convinced beyond doubt that she was not for him. So his feet moved with his will, and his will followed his deeper impulse while his mind told him he was a fool.

He climbed the hill to Danbury, and stayed again at the pond, irresolute, even then half-determined to master his instinct, and go straight on down the long slope into Chelmsford. The wind increased, and the snow fell more thickly. He naturally turned to face the strength of the storm, and almost without knowing it, discovered that he was on the road to Marabella's cottage.

Now he reached the parish boundary, and looked up the track to see if she was visible. The little building, with its roof bowed as it were by the weight of snow and undulating beneath it, showed a single wisp of smoke, and closely shuttered windows. He was about to go towards it and knock, when he saw in the snow the recent impress of a woman's foot.

The direction of the footprints led away from the cottage northwards. As he looked at them he had no doubt in the world that they were made by Marabella; he hesitated but for one moment, and then followed them.

He went to the end of the Ridge, the wind increasing in deep sound and volume about him. When nearly at the northern extremity of the great barrier he stayed, for the marks swung sharply westward. He pursued them amid trees and ever-deepening snow till they ended at the huge bulk of the oak with its gnarled and twisted boughs uplifted against the sky, like a protest from the dying. On the farther side of the bole he came suddenly face to face with the woman he sought.

They seemed alone in the world, these two, and about them the lonely hillside, with its vegetation and coarse growths hidden by the snow, the lowering grey vault above them, the impassive shrill menace of the wind, and trees assembled near by as it were to witness, with a certain aloofness and scorn almost, another little human tragedy.

Beneath his passion, Simon Freeman knew vaguely of these things, but what dominated him was the woman before him – her flushed cheeks, her great, appealing, dark eyes beneath strong brows and flying hair, her red lips parted in wonder, her form swathed beneath her thick cloak, but attracting him, filling him with longing to touch and clasp her.

He caught at his hat, and stood bareheaded for a moment with eyes downcast, as though asking for forgiveness for the strength of his longing. His face was pale, his mouth tightly shut. Lines of trial and discipline were about it, and scored his forehead. He looked at her now with a strange light in his eyes, and spoke to her.

"I have but few words, Marabella. I went from thee, deeming that was thy wish. I cannot forget thee, nor cease to desire thee. In all my life there is nought that is real to me but that thou art absent, and that I long for thy presence."

He stopped lamely, and she felt strangely powerless, as though incapable of realizing her own will, or of using judgement. She noticed, avoiding his gaze, with a curious attention to unimportant details, how the snowflakes fell upon her hair again and dissolved slowly. And then some wave of response broke in her, some need of companionship and protection that somehow she felt was unlawful for her to satisfy,

and she began to weep. Tears rolled down her face, and her breast heaved tumultuously. He came to her, but she put out her hands, holding him off.

"The Strange Woman!" she broke out – "the Strange Woman!" She felt a supreme need of making him understand a gulf fixed between them.

"I will not touch thee, Marabella. Yet I would that thy shelter should be my shelter.... 'Tis a wintry world, and there be few oaks in it that are great enough for us both." He essayed a poor smile.

She made room for him where there was some protection. "'Tis an ill chance that thou'rt here," she said. "Go thy way, the way of a man, and find forgetfulness of unhappiness."

"Ill chance, or God His will, Marabella? I need thee as none other. I will not listen to thy talk of old troubles. Let us go, thou and I and Robin, oversea, to the Virginias, belike. I have sought and not found. Hast thou any secret knowledge that should part us and lift thee nearer to God? What hath the light of the Abyss showed thee?"

She swept the tears from her eyes, and looked at him steadily.

"I am a sinful woman, as I have been. I did think that from the flame, like the tongues of fire in the Scriptures, I might receive remission and the fruits of repentance and the uplifting of Mary Magdalen.... I am thrust back to the old bitterness, and the old name!"

"Yet that did seem not devilry – that glance we had, thou and I, into the Abyss."

"Devilry? No, the edge of the world unseen, as I guess, but not for me, not for me."

"Then wherefore were we led thither? Wherefore to-day here?"

She shuddered helplessly. He thought it was the bitter cold that was chilling her, and took off his cloak, putting it about her shoulders, spite of her protest.

"Surely our own souls bare witness, and the Scripture, and our leading in religion – we are here in the world for God His purpose. And that is what is to come, not what hath been accomplished and is past.... Why, dear woman, what is real to us is not a bitter retrospect, but outlook."

"Some dream of new life did come to me, when I drew into me the fire from the Abyss; new life by way of humbleness and hardness. So I sought it, and do feel mocked – yet I would not blame God..... There was a wondrous beauty, there, in the fire."

"Ay. And a dream of new life came to me also, Marabella. A hope and an impelling to a liberty from the cramped and starved life I had lived before. And I have seen where the wayward will of man leadeth when he maketh a god of his own lust, and persuadeth himself they be the motions of the Spirit."

"God made me a woman; how shall I 'scape suffering therefore?"

"God made me a man – thy mate, Marabella, to lift it from thee and defend thee."

"Thou? Why, thou knowest naught of me – not even who is the father of my child, and what happened then."

"The past – the dead past. Breathe not life into it. I will know naught save thou wilt tell me. Slay the past, Marabella."

"Shall I slay Robin, Simon Freeman? Shall I stop all the tongues that call me 'Strange Woman'?"

He was silent for a while, searching desperately for words to draw her nearer to himself in spirit. The snow had stopped, and the wind blew keener again. The sky lifted, and little sparkles of frost glimmered upon the white surface of the waste. A sinister sound came from above them. The carrion crow had returned and resumed his calling, perched upon a lofty branch.

"Ah, drive it off – the bird of death!" she said, putting her hands to her ears.

"Death? Nay; the creature is mateless."

Freeman stepped out from their refuge, and, waving his hat, drove the bird away.

Marabella laughed pitifully, and the man laughed too. Suddenly her laughter took a wilder note. It continued, and she broke into stormy tears. She thrust out her hands gropingly, and he caught them.

"I am broken and weak.... 'tis unfair!" she cried from below her hood.

Her head was bent and turned from him. He put his arms about her, and held her passionately, seeking her face.

"Thou'rt mine, Marabella. God willeth it."

She lifted her head slowly, and looked with strange intentness at him.

"Doth He then? Wilt judge for us both?"

There was a power that was above them both, and swept them resistlessly in its torrent. Their souls met with a strange shock as she yielded to his kisses.

* * * * *

An impulse rose within them both to gain some spiritual ratification of their new life.

"Let us seek the flame from the Abyss. We have gone astray in the wilderness to find our way home after strange lessons. What hath God to say to this?"

His arm went round her, and they leaned against the old tree, close pressed together. The light waned slowly.

Chapter XXVIII

THE WATCHERS

Walter Raynal, dying in the narrow room with the black beams at the 'Rose and Crown,' was restless. There was a strange quiet about. Not a man was in the place, and there was no drinking in outhouse or cellar. An old woman came in at intervals and looked after him moistening his lips with a feather dipped in water. She could not tell whether or no he was conscious, for his eyes were ever open, gazing mysteriously and changelessly upward. Once he murmured something. She bent to listen and caught the

words:

"So beautiful a face!"

"Whose then, master?"

There was no answer. A hand lifted slightly, as though to point. The woman gazed a while, and departed. She did not return for some time. The room was very quiet. Outside the wind piped over the fallen snow.

Presently, with a terrible deliberation, Raynal sat up in bed. His face took an intense expression, then a sort of horror overspread it. He had a vision.

"Nay," he whispered, "not there, not there!"

Sweat stood upon his forehead, and he fell back again, his face vacuous. Soon he raised himself with the same deliberation, but turned his face in a new direction.

"Come," he said; "come!" Then he relapsed again.

* * * * *

On the broken wall of the ancient earthwork upon the hilltop a huge pile of bracken and dead wood had been gathered by the villagers. Some days ere the snow had fallen,

186

the men, led by Treasure, had gone in a body to the Camp, and with spades and mattocks had build up a sort of platform on the northwestern edge of the oval. The platform was square, of about seven yards extent from side to side, and rose several feet from the level of the ground. Upon this they had reared a beacon, ready for kindling when the word should be given. Despite the snow, it was very inflammable, the wood being mostly rotten; the dead furze and broom in the centre, being protected from the weather, needed but a spark and a breath of air to catch light. The whole structure stood about twenty feet high. The northern side and the summit were crowned with snow, and on the leeward side half a dozen men were gathered, their eyes fixed westward, where stood the heights of Burntwood, whence a signal from London might be seen.

Abel was among them. Although left in charge of the child, he had caught from passers-by what was toward, and he could not resist being a participant in the unusual proceedings. His open mouth and vacant face, his hanging hands and stumbling gait did not pass without comment from the others, but mostly they let him alone. He bore in his hand an old firelock, taken from the hut, with some hazy idea of adding to the celebration by exploding it. Will Treasure flapped his arms about him.

"Should a' tried the King in midsummer," said he. "Then us could keep warm when us joyed for his head bein' cut off."

"They as does it – Bradshaw and them – will be warm enow in hell!" said a fat man with a big beard.

"Silence, man; that's treason now. 'A sold us to the Scots or the Irish or the Dutch, I misremember which. Plague o' kings and all leaders and dukes, I say…. Saul and his spawn…. Then there's Omri, Zimri, and Ahab….. An' do ye consider Solomon. Women an' witty sayings, 'twas all he cared on, besides jackanapes, peafowl, and the long tusks o' behemoth!"

A thin man stamped his feet and wiped his nose. He glanced round and opened his rat-trap of a mouth to speak, but another forestalled him:

"Aw, give tongue a rest, Silas! Push yon faggot wi' thy skinny shoulder. 'Tis a mighty affliction to be thin like thou."

"Prophet or judge, man o' valour or he that hath Jehovah's lips in's ear-hole – Jephthah or Amos – them's the lads to work deliverance!"

"There was a preachin' man at Colchester siege, when I got dinged on the sconce by a misbegotten malignant – this same preachin' man, bein' drunk was a-holdin' for patriarchs with a woundy lot o' wives.... No King, no Parlyment, says he, but each family on's own dunghill, so to say."

The speaker, a lame woodman with a shaggy head, peered through slits of eyes, and wagged his beard, leaning on a staff.

"And what say you to that?"

"False doctrine, and the ploy of the fowl-yard. I did miscall the man for that he was drunk, and he says his spirit was so lofty that it mattered not what's body did. 'Let the beast range and be fed,' says he, 'so that the soul shall have peace from ut, an' look after the things of God!"

"A strange man, neighbour."

"An' no mistake. Says he, that was true interpretation of Scripture doctrine about he that is married caring for the things that shall please his wife, but that he that is unmarried for the things of God. He says, marriage was union o' soul and body, and he would have it slack, as it suited both." The woodman peered westwards and stamped about.

"Any spark o' fire yet, Tammas Lee?"

"Nary glint.... Take thy cursed firelock from my foot, you vagrom Bedlamite!"

Thomas turned furiously to Abel, who nearly fainted with fear and removed hastily. There was little room, as they were all huddled on one side of the beacon, and Abel got edged out into the wind. The cold grew as the darkness increased. Ice

188

formed a crust upon the snow under foot. The sky cleared, and the stars shone with unwonted brilliance in the frost.

"Hast thy lanthorn alight, Job?"

"Ay; my fingers were cold else. Shall us light the sticks and go home to bed? King or Parlyment, God gave us beds and bellies. Flyin' in's Face, I do call it, to go starved and void!.... Would I were with thy wife and thy hogsheads, Will Treasure. A quart of small ale and a log on the fire, say I, and hell take all politics!"

"Nay, th' Colonel saith, 'beacon must be lighted as soon as Burntwood glimmereth, to show our joy at Charles his death,' and here we stay. An' if any man speak of 'King' any more, he shall go into the stocks, by Tollymy, which is a horribly binding oath."

There were grunts of discontent and resignation, stamping of feet, beating of breasts and blowing of fingers. The wind seemed to bite with a keener edge.

* * * * *

Jordan Gyll, priest, strove with painful intensity to fix his mind on his Office. The little room in the ruined house in Wickham Bishops was bitterly cold. He had gone there from Danbury miserably, and intended to disclose all to his superior, but the bishop had gone again, and there were but two or three inmates of the house.

He had seen that Raynal wanted for nothing, and had hoped to bring him away from the inn at Little Baddow, but that was impossible. His mind constantly wandered to the old man with his mysterious ways. He knew now, and shuddered at the thought, that the secret priest who had assisted at his ordination and 'Billy Blind,' the wizard, whom in past years he had suspected of being in unholy league with Marabella and of being a necromancer, were one and the same man.

The revelation which the woman had made before Sir Humphrey Mildmay in the course of her denunciation, that there was a child, his child, living, stirred the man to the deeps of his nature. He must make amends – even at the cost of his priesthood he must make amends – if Marabella would allow.

He pictured her fiercely renouncing all claim upon him, and denying all need of help. She would look terribly beautiful. He recalled their parting, his horror at the thing he thought diabolical, his mother's wild warnings, his panic terror lest his soul were already held and enmeshed, the price he had received for it in the brief love of Marabella..... Could he have done otherwise that go as he did, to seek in wild

penance a reconciliation with God; to offer himself, after long humiliation, as a humble instrument to help others?

He rose from his knees, and thought on Raynal's last monition. Marabella and the stranger to whom he had given the letter were to be stayed from going to the Camp. But where were they, and how was he to act?

And then in the silence, as he closed the book that had been opened at the fifty-first Psalm, he heard a voice he knew, and as he heard, he felt his skin prickle and his hair stir, while his throat choked and drew dry.

"Come," said the voice. "Come!"

He turned, half expecting to see Walter Raynal in the flesh, or an apparition, but the room was void of any being that could be seen.

As in a dream he extinguished the tapers and went down the broken stairway to the dark stables. A horse was there, and with a sort of mechanical precision he saddled it, and rode down the steep hill, slipping in the frozen snow, and making slow progress. It was midnight ere he came to the 'Rose and Crown,' and he tethered his horse to the signpost.

The place was absolutely still. A square of light in the front room showed dimly where the dying man lay. He lifted the latch quietly and entered. The first thing he saw was Will

190

Treasure's wife, profoundly asleep in the settle by the chimney. Her head rested against the wall, and her hands hung down. He turned to the bed.

Walter Raynal's face showed eager excitement. It was grey and colourless, and the brow was damp. The blue eyes still stared upward, and the mouth moved incessantly.

Jordan Gyll, the priest, came to the bedside and knelt, taking the cold hand in his own. He could make nothing of the words the quivering lips were murmuring, yet after a while they came to him.

"Thou'rt come, as I prayed.... Go now.... Stay them.... They are at the Camp, where the fire riseth from the Abyss..... Go now..... Stay them.... At the Camp, where the fire riseth from the Abyss.... God.... Mercy!..."

He ceased, and a look of quietness and peace smoothed the lines in his face. And then slowly the eyes half closed.

Jordan Gyll hesitated. He looked round at the unconscious woman, at the empty room. Then he walked to the door and went out into the night. He bent to the ground and dug away the snow from the turf with his hand. Carefully he plucked three tiny blades of grass and returned. He put them upon the bed, and poured a tiny drop of water into a wooden spoon, laying it beside them. Then he took a Service Book from his pocket. He said the consecration prayer from the Communion over them, and laid two of the grass-blades within Walter Raynal's mouth, using the words of administration; the third he took himself. He poured a drop of water carefully between the parched lips, and finished the remainder himself, using again the words of administration, "The Body of our Lord Jesus Christ, - the Blood of our Lord Jesus Christ."

The old woman in the settle stirred in her sleep as though she dreamed, and her breathing became less stertorous. Walter Raynal gave a little sigh, opened his eyes, closed them again, smiled, and died.

Jordan Gyll paused a moment and then stepped quietly to the door, unlatching it, and, closing it behind him, passed down the path to the sign. He loosed his horse and rode northward. The wind blew his wide-brimmed hat back from his brows, and as he caught it to pull it forward he had a glimpse, far away, of a bright light burning upon a hill.

Chapter XXIX

BURNT SACRIFICE

It was dusk when Simon Freeman and Marabella turned into the Ridge track close to the windmills. In the minds of both of them there was the vague thought of bringing the new offering of their resolve and love to the altar where they had been brought into closest touch with the spiritual world. Whatever civil or religious ceremony might be undertaken subsequently, this visit to the Camp, where the light of the world invisible had enveloped them, and the life of it entered into them, should be the spiritual bond.

They were conscious of being overruled by a Fate that had caused them to live their mortal lives contemporaneously, had trained and disciplined them by strange circumstances, had brought them together by a strange association of events, and had led them to drink of the same mysterious fount under the tutelage of the same hierophant. They spoke of him, 'old Billy Blind,' as Marabella called him, and Freeman told her what he knew of him. Suddenly he stopped.

" 'Tis as though he were here," he said. "Dost feel the like, Marabella?"

"Ay," she said; " 'tis because we speak of him. Let us go on."

He put his arm about her, and they went forward slowly, bending their heads against the keen wind. They turned eastward, and came to the edge of the waste. She caught at him and pointed.

"I saw a man yonder, waving his arms at us," she whispered. "Yet I do not see him now…. A little man with a cloak…. Almost I thought it was he."

"Who, child?"

"Billy Blind. Yonder, under the holly. Perchance he hath gone behind it. I am somewhat afeared."

"Nay, we who seek the fire of the other world as friends seek a home, as refugees seek a Stronghold, need fear no fancies."

"A Stronghold.... Yes, thy love is a Stronghold to me, as mine to thee. They drive us – the cruelties and griefs of life – and thus we 'scape them. The world of spirits – of life's desire, calleth us and shall give us – what?"

"Vision, and a greater life. We hallow our love, the union of souls within That which unites, or so I think; and then – home, Marabella."

"The cottage?" She shrank closely to him, her face hidden. "A wintry home-coming, love," she whispered.

"Nought's needed but thee," he answered.

"Leave all to me. What shall let us now?"

She peered out again into the dusk. "Look yonder, again," she said. "There, by the holly – 'tis he, surely!"

"I see nought but shadows. We will go thither, if thou wilt."

They came to the spot beneath the tree. The snow was spread white and stainless all about it.

"Thou seest: there be no footmarks."

She stared at the snow, perplexed. "Nevertheless, I think he was here," she said. "He spread his arms, thus."

Darkness gathered, and they paused once and again to be sure of the way to the old earthwork on the hilltop. The world was fallen silent, and there was little wind now. Snow dislodged itself from the bare branches or leaves of the evergreens as they passed. Rabbits darted across their way, leaving tiny footprints.

Presently the trees ceased, and they came to open space, where the ruined walls of earth rose upon the crest of the hill. At the farther edge rose the great pile of the beacon, but is was scarce visible in the darkness. Beyond it there was a vague indefiniteness blending sky and landscape in shadow.

194

"The Camp," said Freeman. "Dost see the oak on the barrow?"

They moved on together over the low wall. Soon they stood before the long mound beneath the tree, looking at one another through the gloom. Moved by common impulse, they mounted the barrow and knelt upon the snow.

"Let us think on those whose bodies lie beneath," said Freeman in a low tone. "They live, bound by That which maketh them one – twin flames within a fire. By their power have we been led to one another. The gift is their gift to us. God hath bid them speak of Him and give for Him."

They remained kneeling together for a while, but there was no sign. A vague murmur as of voices came from the direction of the beacon. The two held one another tightly.

"Didst hear aught?"

"Thy heart beating, beloved.... Nay, wait. If no answer be given, 'twill mean that we have already had it."

They waited in the darkness, the snow about them, the wind making a sound in the branches of the tree above them as though grieving.

* * * * *

All the watchers by the beacon, save Will Treasure and Abel, slept, wrapped in their cloaks. They had brought liquor to keep themselves warm, and it had had its effect upon them. Treasure had been amusing himself by working upon the half-witted lad's fears with strange tales about the place where they were, and, but for the darkness and the fear of loneliness, Abel would have fled the spot for ever.

Not daring to move, he found small comfort in clutching his firelock and staring out in the direction of Burntwood, whence the signal might be expected.

"Ay," said Treasure, "here it were they fought and slew one another in the owld days, and their bownes lie beneath, some

195

deep and some so fleet A could rise 'em by the strowke of a mattock.... Maybe thou'rt settin' on top of one of them!"

He brought the lanthorn round and pretended to look. Abel moved hastily, his mouth open and his eyes staring.

"An' if ye come at th' right time, ye see 'em – scores of 'em, risin' and fightin' again. One lot swarmin' up yon slope, wi' shields above their 'eds, and another lot within the wall dealin' mighty blows.... What's that?"

"Voices, master.... There be the ghosts comin'!"

Abel caught at Treasure's arm, trembling. The man hid the lanthorn swiftly.

"Keep silence, ye fool! Us'll see who they be; don't, they'll let us alone. We be on King's business – that is, on Parlyment's."

They were silent, hearing no more. Abel's teeth chattered with cold and fear. He stared out into the darkness, and his discomfort, bodily and mental, grew. His feet, wet with the snow that silted through his leaky boots, were numb with cold. His fears would not let him even attempt to sleep, and he had had no artificial soporific like the others. Nevertheless, he closed his eyes and longed for the moment to come when the beacon should be lighted and the others awakened. Dully he thought of Robin asleep in the cottage. If Marabella should return and find the child alone, what would she say? And where was she?...

A sort of inarticulate groan from Treasure awoke him, panic-stricken, to his surroundings.

"O my God!" moaned Treasure; "what's yon?"

Abel stared out. He was no longer encircled by pitchy darkness. The snow, the piled beacon, the trees, the sprawling forms of his companions, were faintly illuminated by an unearthly light. It lay upon the earthwork and the smooth levels like dawn, yet with a strange, rosy intensity, a thickening of the coloured air, as though it had a substance and vitality of its own, or drew it out of whatever it fell upon.

196

He looked fearfully at Treasure. The man was sitting beside him in the lee of the beacon, his eyes projecting, his mouth open; and he was staring at something behind Abel, the source of the strange light.

Abel turned at last toward the barrow. Upon its summit stood a man and a woman clasped together, their faces turned upwards and away from him. A pale flame encircled them both, arising apparently from the ground. At its base it was of a pure golden colour, but the edges were tipped with rose. It broke into lesser flames and wrapped them about, and it disseminated itself in fiery flakes and cloudy mist into the atmosphere about them. There was no sound, but the scene was awful in its beauty: the

snow, the flame, the vast firmament, the empty spaces....

He felt the sweat run down him, and his hands clutched his neighbour. He babbled without finding words.

Something of their terror found its way through the beclouded faculties of the other men. They woke and stared, and struggled to their feet, cursing and praying. They turned to run, and had started when the sound of a horse's hoofs, struggling up the steep slope below, stayed them.

" 'Tis the devil's self, come for yon wizards!" cried one man in a strangled voice. They shrank back, huddling together at the beacon's foot.

The rosy light increased, and as the watchers stared, the man and the woman spread their hands upwards. A strange answering light seemed to descend delicately and mingle with the rising flame....

Abel, clutching at the ground, his face buried in snow, felt his hand clasp something cold. He clawed it without knowing what it was, and then a vague thought found its way through his paralysed brain. He drew his fingers along the barrel of his old firelock, and pulled it towards him. He brought himself to look again at the fearful spectacle of abominable wizardry, and then thrust the gun towards Treasure.

The man grasped it. He was the only one who even attempted to control himself. The others were all in a state of helpless and insane panic. He pointed the firelock toward the strange apparition, the sweat falling from his brows into his eyes, hindering his aim. The barrel shook, and he laid it upon a boulder. Then he made the sign of the cross over it, aimed once more, and fired.

A wild explosion shattered the air and went echoing around the hills followed. Instantaneously there was pitchy darkness. The appearance of the man and woman, the rose light, the mist, the flames, suddenly were not. The watchers clung together. Below them, whence the sound of the horse had proceeded, there was a plunging, a cry, and a crash.

"Light, for Christ's sake!" cried Treasure hoarsely. "The lanthorn!"

It was found somewhere and fumbled with. He seized it, jangled, and thrust it into the base of the beacon, where a hollow was prepared, sheltered, and made ready with pitch and shavings to catch fire more easily. There was a spluttering and a crackle, followed by a great humming sound as the flame drove into the centre of the pile. Then, like a strange winged being, it climbed the side of the beacon, touching the edges of the projecting twigs and bracken and making them break forth into a sort of dreadful flowering.

The fire spread right and left. Spurts and jets of flame leapt out and up. A dense smoke poured forth and, driven by the wind, enveloped the men. Forced by the suffocating clouds and the intolerable heat, they retreated, their faces turning continually toward the barrow, which was by this time brightly illuminated. One old man was lifted with difficulty from his knees to his feet. He had been praying frenziedly. Another fled from his companions and ran at his utmost speed from the spot, his mouth open, his eyes staring. Treasure found something kicking and struggling at his feet in the snow as he moved away from the beacon, trying to keep the men together. It was Abel in an epileptic seizure. None tended him, and presently his struggles ceased.

By now the terrific roar of the beacon had increased so that speech between the watchers was difficult. The wind fanned the flames, and blew them over the men's heads like great wings. The snow hissed as it melted about the pile for yards, and ever and anon enormous clouds of sparks sprang from the summit.

Soon the dense smoke grew less, and the beacon appeared almost pure flame, casting a dazzling light for a great way. The men, with infinite caution and keeping close together, approached the barrow.

Treasure pointed. Freeman, shot through the heart, lay twisted curiously upon the mound, and beside him Marabella lay dead also. The heavy bullet had passed through her lover and entered her breast. Her dark hair was spread over his face, and her head rested upon his shoulder.

"Warlocks," said the old man tremblingly. "They'll walk and haunt the place without ye stake 'em!"

"Nay," said Treasure, " 'twill be as well if we put 'em into the fire."

"Then do thou the work, for touch 'em will not I…. God, how hot it is!"

"Go thou, Aaron, and deal wi' em."

The man came close to the barrow and stared at the bodies.

"Nay, my feyther were Anabaptist. Doubt if I be christen'd. Leave them there and go home, say I."

Treasure strode to the summit of the mound. His face showed his dread as he stooped and turned the body of the woman over. Her face was strangely peaceful, and the eyes were half closed; the lips, slightly stained with blood, were parted as though to welcome something.

He wrapped her in his cloak and beckoned a man authoritatively to take the feet. They carried the body as near to the beacon as they could go for the heat, and laid it upon the ground. Then they returned and took up the body of Freeman, laying it by the side of Marabella. Retreating hastily from the fierce heat, they cleansed their hands in snow. A wallet with money in it was left on the ground, and Freeman's sword had become loosed, but strong as was their cupidity, no one would keep them. They were hurled

into the fire.

"Sere wood from the other side!" said Treasure.

They flocked round to the other side of the beacon, and tore down some faggots, piling them on the top of the bodies. Then they brought a brand and fired the smaller pyre.

Soon the beacon grew top-heavy. The flames had roared their way through the base, and the whole structure tilted. With a crash and a terrific volume of sound and flame, the beacon fell upon the newly piled faggots. A volcano of sparks and smoke spouted upwards.

"Liquor, for God His love!" cried one man.

But they had left it at the foot of the wood-pile in their fear. They wiped their brows and surveyed one another.

Then, without further words, they turned and went in a body, holding fast to each other as they went through the snow, breathing heavily. They left the flaming mass and drove into the darkness. As they reached the Ridge and their eyes grew more accustomed to the light, they descried, far and near, other beacons alight upon the Essex hilltops.

Not a man went to his own home save Treasure. They all went to the 'Rose and Crown,' and flung themselves down in one room, talking in whispers. Treasure's wife drew him apart.

"Billy Blind be dead," she said. " 'A died while I was asleep. Wilt see him?"

"Nay; have seen enow. Am like a leaf we' ague..... Get us all some strong waters!...

He went and joined his companions.

"Neighbours, not a word o' this night's doings. If any man speak of it, I, Will Treasure, will stab him with my own hand."

He glowered at them all, and they swore, readily enough, that they would keep silence.

So the death of the King was proclaimed from the old Camp on the hilltop at Little Baddow.

Chapter XXX

ASHES

Jordan Gyll faced the winter night, pulling his cloak close and flinging it about his shoulders, blowing upon his fingers, and kicking his heels at his horse's sides. The beast stumbled and slid over the vile track, made worse by snow partly frozen and partly dissolved into the deep ruts and holes left by carts.

He had but a vague idea what he was to do, yet he hesitated not a whit. The command of the dead man lay strongly upon him. He was to stay Freeman and Marabella in some project upon which they were engaged, even now, at the Camp upon the hilltop. His mind jumped to the conclusion that the flame and the Abyss were in some way connected with what he himself had witnessed years ago. Then he had fled from Marabella; now he was to save her, in a manner not yet revealed to him.

He swung easterly at the forge, and made the best pace he could, past Holy Bread Farm and on to the foot of the hill. Then he climbed a space, leading his horse, and mounted him again as he left the rough road that followed an old watercourse down the hillside, and struck easterly again along a path that led beside the darkness and impenetrable mystery of Scrub Wood, and on to the waste of the Warren, whence the Camp hill rose above the brook, swollen now with the snow. Fallen timber stayed him, and brambles grew over the wretched path. He forded the brook and extricated his horse from the marsh that took its hoofs fetlock-deep. He arrived at the base of the hill and there stayed.

An unearthly light rose from the summit. He could see the bold lines of the ancient Stronghold at the crown of the steep scarp. He saw with wonder the great pile of the beacon, as yet unlighted, on the verge of the enclosure, and from it moved vague forms, crying and gesticulating....

With something between a sob and a prayer, he set his horse at the rough ascent. It sprang forward in answer to spur and blow, and struggled upward, scattering pebbles and sods behind. More terribly laboured came its breath, yet the summit was near. The man's mind held but one thought, to reach the centre and source of the strange illumination, and there to call upon God to vindicate or defeat this terrible manifestation to which the man and the woman he was to rescue had yielded themselves. As for these others, crying and gesturing beside a huge pile, what were they? Devils?...

A sudden loud explosion rolled along the hills. His horse reared, swerved sideways down the slope, made a frantic effort to recover, and overbalanced, falling backwards. Jordan Gyll tried instinctively to avoid being fallen upon, and half succeeded. He was aware of a crash, as of the world in ruins about him, a sense of anger and despair, and then there was void and darkness.

* * * * *

It was daybreak when his senses came back to him slowly, first with an aching in his limbs, and then with pain in his eyes where blood had run in them and congealed. He pieced his memories together wonderingly, trying to discover what his purpose had been, and what had led to his lying there. He raised himself to a sitting posture and swept his eyes clear. Close to him lay his horse, dead, with a broken back. He stared at it and, with a rush, reality came to him.

With pain he rose, disencumbering himself from cloak and stirrups, marvelling at the way in which he had fallen clear of the horse that had neither kicked nor rolled on him. A sickening smell of smouldering peat was about him, and, looking upward, he saw a wisp of blue smoke beaten downhill by the wind and coming from the place where he had seen the pile. He realised that he had lain all night, and that the beacon had been lit and had burned itself out. He climbed slowly and stiffly toward it, bending forward.

He reached the top. The marks of many feet were printed in the snow. They went from the beacon to the barrow and back again. The pile was reduced to a huge heap of grey ashes with a blue reek issuing from it. Ever and anon a puff of wind caught the ashes and blew the surface into the air, where they travelled a little way and then fell, to define the snow. The man went slowly to the barrow. The white surface of the snow was disturbed and broken by many footprints, and in the midst of it was a dark stain

of blood. He went back to the trampled base of the beacon. A heap of half-consumed wood broke into flame, fanned by the wind that blew stronger with the coming of the dawn. He moved away from the flying smoke, and passed round to leeward of the ash-pile.

The form of a youth, sprawling half in snow and half under wooden billets, lay before him. It was Abel. He bent and turned the face upward. A deep wound upon the forehead, where the hair was matted darkly, showed where the wood had fallen upon him as he lay helpless in his seizure. Jordan Gyll felt at the boy's heart. A faint movement was discernible. He dragged him away and chafed the limp hands, bathing the brow with snow, and wrapping his own cloak about the helpless body. Presently, in response to his efforts, the eyes rolled upon and stared vacantly.

"Who be you?"

"A minister: what hath happed?"

"Happed? Why?... 'Tis mortal cold. Where be I?"

"At the Camp, by the beacon. Didst light it? Where are the other men?"

The empty look on Abel's face changed swiftly to a look of horror. He choked and shrank away from Gyll.

"Art another wizard – come for my soul?... I did not slay 'em.... 'Twas Will Treasure fired the shot!"

Jordan Gyll's eyes travelled to the dark stain on the barrow. 'Slay them? Slay whom?... Where are Marabella and Freeman?"

"Dead and damned! Dead and damned! and their bodies cast into the burning fiery furnace.... My sister the witch and her leman.... Dead and damned!"

Gyll felt an awful chill grow at his heart. Existence suddenly took an aspect of hopeless and purposeless tragedy. He stared dreadfully at the ash-heap. Somewhere there.... His face contorted with the thought.

"Tell me," he whispered. "Thou art Abel – I recall thee, Marabella's brother. Where lived she?"

"Ah, sir, take I home. Cottage on the Ridge by Danbury bound.... My head!"

The boy's eyes rolled, and his lips had a light foam about them. He struggled in another seizure. Gyll held him till he became quiet. The scene and the circumstances seemed like a wild and fantastic dream. He refused to admit the reality of it all, lest he should madden.

He picked up the boy and strode a little way. The form lay a dead weight within his arms. Suddenly his breath came stertorously, with pauses between each respiration. Gyll looked quickly at him and laid him down on the edge of the earthwork upon his cloak. In a minute his breathing ceased, and the vacant face took on a look of peace and secret wisdom. He was dead.

The man gazed dumbly at him, and stared round again at the beacon. He slowly retraced his steps, as though drawn by an irresistible power. He came to the ashes, with the blue smoke rising against the white world below a grey sky, and groped with strange intensity among them. His hands blackened and became foul with the charred wood and flaky dust. He threw aside billets and embers, the twisted framework of a lanthorn, a piece of iron that might once have been a sword. The sweat poured down his face, and he choked with the flying ask and dust. His hands were burned with the hot core of the pyre, as the little flames sprang up from half-consumed fuel where the draught breathed life into the smoulder.

At length his hand closed upon a black molten object that he knew of old. It was the brooch with which Marabella was used to fasten her cloak. He recalled loosing it, his arm about her.... It was attached to a fragment of cloth, and within a corner of it that had escaped the fierce conflagration were a few poor fragments, charred and shattered, the relics of what was once Marabella's beauty. He drew them out and fell upon the snow beside them, in an agony of weeping.

* * * * *

A gale blew that morning, and as it subsided, drowning rain fell and a sudden thaw set in. Jordan Gyll, coming that afternoon to the hilltop once more with Will Treasure and old Silas unwillingly in his wake, found the snow well-nigh gone. The two men who followed bore a hurdle, and upon it the body of Abel was laid, and moreover a folded cloak that they did not open. In silence they began their journey to the churchyard. Whatever each man conjectured as to the thoughts of his companions, at least they spake no word one to another. With their native reticence they proceeded imperturbably to their task.

The bearers went slowly down the slope, and Jordan Gyll turned to give a last look at the scene – the earthwork with a fast-disappearing covering of snow, the barrow, the remains of the beacon, with puffs of ashes flying from its summit in the strong gale.

Suddenly he became immovable. A tiny figure was moving slowly towards him on the southern edge of the Camp. He observed it curiously and with some awe. It was a little child, a boy, and he was gazing intently at the ground. Presently Jordan Gyll saw what he was doing. He was tracking footprints, setting his own in them as he reached them. The tracks led straight to the barrow.

In a flash Jordan understood. Marabella's child – his child – had followed his mother, using the footprints as a clue. Along the Ridge, with the intense carefulness of a child with a single idea, he had followed them; to the oak, further still, to the Camp – and now?...

The man went forward and stood before the child. He was a pathetic little figure, bare-headed, with unshod feet that were blue with cold. His hair streamed in the rough wind, and tears stood upon his cheeks. Clad simply in his night-rail, he thrust out his hands appealingly, like the Christ-child, outcast in a wintry world.

Jordan Gyll took him up. The blue eyes looked with simple inquiry into his own. Then, apparently satisfied, the boy nestled into the man's arms and went to sleep on his shoulder.

The two followed the hurdle as it was borne slowly toward the grey tower of the church.

THE END

38565414R00126

Made in the USA
Charleston, SC
10 February 2015